THE POEMS

ISBN: 978-1-916541-12-2

First edition.

First published in 2025 by Erratum Press
Sheffield, UK
www.erratumpress.com

Design and typesetting by Ansgar Allen

THE POEMS
a novella

William Walsh

ERRATUM PRESS

The poem belonged to everyone. The poem came into being through a magical process that was impossible to replicate, even under ideal laboratory conditions. The poem began life in a flowerpot. The poem was not about birth. The poem was about gestation. The poem's parents were poems. In utero, the poem was attached to two placentas. The poem had two navels at birth. The poem was born of frustration. The poem was born of heartache. Every cell in the poem's body was a poem. The poem was out of the cradle, endlessly rocking. The poem learned how to crawl. The poem's diaper was full. The poem's first baby-steps were witnessed by an audience of cats. The poem baby-stepped into a new genre. The poem cultivated a cult following. The poem invented love. The poem was lovelier than a tree. The poem contained the full curriculum of a middle school health and hygiene course. The poem detailed how babies were made. The poem knew how to clear a room. The poem refined amok. The poem studied rules of verse. The poem bruised easily. The poem looked up at the moon and just knew. The poem was woven into a green screen fabric. The poem's TED Talk "On Whispering" was misheard by millions. The poem could be deployed as a pickup line as well as a put down. Like money in the bank, over time the poem earned interest. The poem's startled lens captured the internal anxiety under the surface of every face. The poem knew all there was to know about anxiety. The poem enacted decay, gave legs to decadence. The poem was corrupted. The poem enforced a rule of brutal honesty. The poem was a hermit crab story. The poem was a shaggy dog story. The poem was a mongrel's doggerel. The poem was a sob story. The poem made a listicle. There wasn't a selfish bone in the poem's body. The poem was living through dark times and singing songs about dark times. The poem was invented in spring. The poem was an invincible summer. The poem's fall was inevitable. The poem was institutionalized in the winter. The poem had the metric consistency of a tattoo artist's pen. The poem was shorthand for love's sweet and musical wistfulness. What pressed so on the beating heart of the poem? The poem noted that a jet's highest decibel level is generally in the range of 115 dB, while some rock bands played at 130 dB. The poem was a June bug versus a hurricane. The poem located its abjective correlative in a sapped teabag. The poem found love in a hopeless place. The poem's nose was as sharp as that of a drug sniffing canine. The poem couldn't sit still. The poem was lost in love. The poem was lost in lust. The poem had lust issues. The poem saw no reason to get out of bed. The poem felt a plank in reason break. The poem was silly on the surface. The poem's heart was in the right place. The poem was a spiked punch at a high school dance. The poem was a gut punch at a middling fraternity. The poem was a punch to the solar plexus in a dive bar. The poem drove like a bootlegger. The poem, a ginger, feared being slapped on the street on November 10th each year. The poem howled at the moon. The poem bayed at the moon. The poem blamed everything on the moon. The poem was about the house like a cat. The poem had no haptics, no iron in its blood. The poem was a cross between a fox and the hedgehog. The poem married an essay on government to form a hybrid text. The poem was exhausted at the center of an orgy. The poem spewed a word-stew. The poem tossed a word-salad. The poem had lost some teeth to years of gnawing. The poem had sturm. The poem had drang. The poem wore a cape and some fake plastic fangs. The poem's childhood was hell. All day, the poem tried to distinguish news from desire. The poem was a weighted blanket. The poem was graffiti. The poem, like paradise, was a kind of library. The poem had balls that hung lower than Mick Fleetwood's on the cover of the *Rumours* album. The poem liked all of Nirvana's pretty songs. In order to get as drunk as a chumbawamba, the poem took a whiskey drink, then a vodka drink, then a lager drink, and then a cider drink. The poem was truly tubthumpingly drunk, singing "Danny Boy" and insisting that everyone else in the pub sing along. The poem was pissing the night away. Several times, the poem got knocked down, but each time the poem got back up again. The poem was winning. The poem was intermittently vegan. The poem was a good deal of joy and pain and wonder, with a dash of the dictionary. The poem was the hole in an adder stone. Surrender was the poem's greatest weapon. The poem was an endless archive. The poem's whole life was like a picture of a sunny day. The poem saw cows in the pasture, two by two. The poem owed a debt to the real. The poem witnessed a crime with no voice, just hands in mime. The poem was disarming. The poem was unarmed. The poem fell into the arms of Venus de Milo. The poem was a sinner. The poem was a compost pile. The poem's boat was written on water. The poem was in a high boat with a short oar. The poem's oars were afraid of water. The poem was a boat that forgot how to float. The poem was an engine of transference. The poem had the look of royalty. On the page, the poem resembled discombobulation. The poem was a collective, a co-op, a commune, a kibbutz. The poem was a big tent. The poem was a speed walker. The poem always went up a flight of stairs two steps at a time. The poem was a bounder. The poem left tracks for others to follow. The poem was a feature-length animated movie. The poem was a weather report. The poem was a reflex camera. The poem was an A-frame house. In dreams, the poem walked alone. The poem's heart had more than four chambers. The poem was stuck in the 'fail better' part of trying again. The poem was exceptional when it came to preparing for failure. The poem admitted to forgery but was in no way a plagiarist. Appropriation freed the poem. The poem dined on allusion. The poem knew of three ways to achieve ultimate success: 1. Be kind. 2. Be kind. 3. Be kind. The poem was an antidote to cynicism. The poem was like thick mayonnaise on a thin sandwich. The poem had no thesis. The poem had no hood to beat the cold wind. The poem had no direction home. The poem reverse-engineered sin to create virtue. The poem tried hard to recreate what had yet to be created. The poem monetized hearsay. The poem deflated thought balloons in comic strips, puncturing the interior life of favorites like, Peanuts, Garfield, Doonesbury, to name but a few. The poem crafted an ending that was endless. The poem kept secrets. The poem was a baptism against all iniquity. A metal-detector found the poem in an overgrown vacant lot near an old shopping center. The poem was a still point in a turning world. The poem changed its cones and rods. The poem was a know-it-all. The poem was a forget-me-not. The poem was a cornucopia of corny aphorisms. The poem had many tributaries. The poem felt the pulse of the morning sun, which was like a drumming. The poem was a long bridal veil. The poem was a natural athlete. The poem had fists of steel. The poem was not just the carcass but the spark. The poem's maximum balanced stress load was akin to that of a Bactrian camel. The poem asked, What if? The poem let it all hang out. The poem was addressed directly to the Pope. The Pope quoted the poem in a sermon that was broadcast across all of Latin America. The poem was a psalm. The poem was a balm. The poem had an otherworldly interior calm. The poem thrived in a caste system. The poem was ever in search of a shorter sentence. The poem required ideal conditions to make love. The poem boiled it all down to cheap talk, patter, and jive. The poem sucked on the lunar lozenge of love. The poem was the life of the party. The poem refused to let the party end. The poem revived a bygone era. The poem taught a dog how to bark and a cat to say, Excuse me. The poem was formed of data and distributed in an agreeable shape via a suitable domain. The poem was a perilous carnival ride. The poem engaged in unsafe sex. The poem was the punctum. About suffering, the poem was never wrong. The poem was an unsuccessful abortion. The poem showed contempt for the contemptible. The poem embodied the paradox of the slut—at once loved and reviled. The poem's apologies were always quite professional, thorough, and absolutely sincere. The poem begged to be reread. The poem had a kind face. The skin of the poem was denim. A sequined gown clothed the poem. The poem was enrobed in chocolate and could be consumed in one bite. The poem was a delicious treat for the ears. The poem was self-destructive. The poem savored the moment of figurative detonation. The poem was not pretty on the page, but it was beautiful when read aloud. The poem believed an incomplete sentence was still a sentence, provided it made sense. The poem was friendless. Recited properly, the poem was an incantation. The poem was a Nintendo cheat code. The poem was a chatbot. The poem provided excellent customer service. The poem was a foreign film—so foreign that it was foreign in every country on Earth. The poem was a jackal. The poem was for the birds. The poem hid its light under a bushel basket. Some force, or pattern of forces, marked the poem at birth and set in motion a second life—and a third after that—with no end in sight, no last generation or final regeneration to be seen. The poem was the lone surviving member of a microgeneration that sprung up between cholera epidemics toward the end of the previous century. The poem was a fragment, yet ever so prosaic. Though the poem was a fragment, it was not incomplete. There was a vastness to the poem's soul. The poem was a scientific self-corrector. The poem reached beyond its sphere of influence. The poem used the word immeasurable when there was no way to calculate the size or weight or dimension of an object or emotion. The poem fit on a bumper sticker. The poem dilly-dallied. The poem was righteous. Like a river, the poem fed a lake. The poem went on and on about the importance of brevity. The poem was a skunk. The poem included well-aimed lines of scorn, abhorrence, and derision. The poem was a Catherine wheel. The poem was a catapult. The poem was a fixture at May Day celebrations, recited by memory as children danced around maypoles. It was more than just a knowledge of words that distinguished the poem. The face of the poem remained unaged for centuries. The poem had two beating hearts. The poem was half as tall as most men and twice as wide across the shoulders. The poem subverted decades worth of longing. The poem longed for a broken heart so bad. The poem's supreme subject was love in all its facets. The poem was a stinging nicotine patch. The poem did not shy away from debate. The poem was engaged with the language but not enslaved to it. Revered or reviled, the poem didn't care which. The poem rebelled against outmoded social pieties. The poem railed against the proposed rerouting of the railroad. The poem raged against the dying of the light. The sky was never blue enough for the poem. The poem had a synthetic feel. The poem was a stilted jeremiad. Those readers who had not yet read the poem knew it by its reputation as a much-vaunted poem. The poem was an emissary. The poem was rapid in movement, simple in style, plain in language, natural in thought, and, above all, noble. The poem was humble to a degree. As policy, the poem never said no to wine. The poem was a silent auditor. The poem thought up adult coloring books years before they came on the market. The poem rounded upon itself to end where it began. The poem was a kingpin, the big cheese. The poem's sense of honor was highly situational. The poem said, Havoc isn't a plan, but it is an effective tactic. The poem said, Chaos isn't a plan, but it can be an effective strategy. The poem was into chaos. The poem was a collection of antiques and curios. The poem projected a privacy shield at public events. The poem was remote, gazeful and gazed upon. The poem was a thorough tongue bath. The poem knew a little bit about a lot of things. The declarative sentence was the poem's bread and butter. The poem gave body to the imperative, to necessary action. The poem was written in an interrogative mood. The poem used the exclamatory reservedly. The poem consumed self-help books by the dozen. The poem was referenced in many a self-help book. The poem was a series of errands. The poem was a passive security restraint. The poem was an uncashed check. The poem had a late breakfast at an egghouse off the interstate. The baby's tantrum was in service to the poem. The poem sired cadence and cascade. The poem had technique and style in equal measure. The poem was a forest fire of indiscretion. The poem was an alarm clock that ran fast. There was, perhaps, too much joy in the poem's life. The poem's inspiration originated in Scotland and it was twelve years old and it came in a shapely bottle. The poem was a geological study and as such was in no great hurry. The poem was first an untamable filly and then a difficult mare. The poem applied makeup to cover a periorbital hematoma. Over time, the poem developed an unerring shame index. In the courtroom of public opinion, the poem litigated a case of fraud perpetrated by a ne'er-do-well. The poem's chorus was a summation of its defense, and it was catchy as hell. The poem, vindicated yet again, uncorked champagne. In a prior life, the poem took the form of three rocks on a beach. The poem was pegged in the head with a lawn dart. The poem was a shit stirrer. The poem scratched on the eight ball. The poem picked up a 7 - 10 split for a nifty spare. The poem was an archive of longing. The poem pressed its own mute button. The poem was pouting again about some imagined slight. The poem was lengthening its stride. The poem was fairly leaping. The poem was an aggregator. The poem's first language was touch. The poem was in danger of becoming silly. The poem set fire to the rain. Money didn't look like money in the poem's hands. The poem dimmed its screen, went into low-power mode. The poem was written with a feather quill on parchment fine. The poem credited all successes to the quill. The poem was typed on a humming IBM Correcting Selectric II. The poem was processed on a word processor, published in an online journal. The poem was scrawled on the men's room wall at Boston's Logan Airport. The poem yawned, open mouthed, at the Grand Canyon. The poem's yawns were always grand. The poem practiced such a subtle form of conformity that it went undetected by a generation of readers. The poem went through a purgation, a retched spell of heaving and aspirating before being granted entrance to heaven. The poem gave names to rainbows like the national weather service dubbed hurricanes. The poem examined the difference between Judy Garland's rendition of "Somewhere Over the Rainbow" sung at age sixteen versus forty-seven. Color-blind, the poem turned its back to the rainbow. The poem framed many verses in situations of this verse versus that verse. The poem lived its life in public, like a frog. The poem had a flair for the obvious. The poem blew through a bleak December wind. The poem resolved itself into a few indelible words. The poem was open to its opposite. The poem remembered everything. The poem had total recall of all things that mattered. The poem had good credit. The poem was elected, not selected. The poem was a remedy but not a cure. The poem was a blunderbuss. The poem was a two-trigger combination rifle/shotgun. The poem was a peashooter. The poem fetishized the reload. Computer analysis of the poem determined it was accessible to readers with a sixth-grade reading comprehension level. The force of the poem's blows was cumulative. The poem recognized its mighty purpose.

The poem knew of a formula, verbal, oral, synaptic. The poem murdered a roast beef sandwich. The poem saved a salad to eat after the main course. The poem was young but had a matronly air. The poem served on a federal grand jury that indicted a ham sandwich. Fire was the poem's favorite technology. The poem risked ruin. The poem's penis was more or less an isthmus, a craggy isthmus. Instinctively, the poem played possum. The poem was a stormbird, a harbinger. The poem contributed a verse to the powerful play that goes on and on. After a long jungle run, the poem's feet were caked with mud. The poem led a rebellion against itself. Come October, and the poem turned the maple's leaves to gold. The poem had good feet. The poem had fast feet. The poem was fleet of foot. The poem never put a foot wrong. The poem drained into a rangy catchment area. The poem was not written in code. The poem knew many wild, wild nights. Once it was clear to everyone on Earth that someone had to be normal, the poem volunteered. The poem knew war. There had been no real peace in the poem's lifetime, and the historical accounts of peace written before the poem's birth seemed, to the poem, to be fantasy. The poem was written in defense of the clip-on necktie, which has been undeservedly maligned. The poem used acting exercises to warm up—sense memory. The poem was a gambler. Chance, fueled the poem, low-stakes, fuck-all chance. Yes, the poem was a chancer. The poem's gift to the world was a single line about sharing a taxi ride that transported readers through the streets of a dozen cities. It was a wonder the poem survived in this world. The poem wore penny loafers. The poem wore a windbreaker. The poem put on an anorak. The poem donned mittens and scarf. The poem slipped into fishnet tights, gravity boots, a micro-miniskirt, and a tight baby t-shirt. The poem wore a blue Oxford shirt and a paisley tie. Chinos were the poem's preferred pants. A pashmina completed the poem's ensemble. A banana skin on the floor of the kitchen was sure evidence a monkey was about the house, and, no doubt, the poem believed, presaged that some monkey business was soon to come. The poem was damn good with a yo-yo, literally and figuratively. The poem was now in the public domain. The poem was intentionally comical in parts, which caused readers to misread the serious bits. The poem was presented as a proof of concept. The poem was written in the language of intensity. Tea was never hot enough in the poem's mouth. The poem and the pastoral. The poem and the underworld. The poem and the knickknack. The poem and the paperweight. The poem and the asterism. The poem and the gnome. The poem and the candle. The poem and the perpetrator. The poem experienced the process of its thinking. The poem was a five-tool athlete of no sport at all. The poem detested July—every day of it. Invariably, the poem vacationed in August. The poem cursed the moon—it was that time of the month. The poem had a lunar fixation. The poem was made of blue cheese. The poem psychically willed the cow to jump over the moon. The poem heard the little dog laugh at seeing such sport. The poem witnessed the dish running away with the spoon. The poem was progressive and digressive in equal parts. The poem was a perfume, intoxicating, unforgettable, slippery, shapeshifting. The poem excised the unexcisable. The poem provided short-term debt relief. The poem would not stop for death. The poem had a soft spot for practicing alcoholics. The poem was a womanizer, but there was a mitigating backstory that must be known. The poem knew some things. The poem was a bit of a show off. The poem's origin story was a variant on every other origin story. The poem was born of two midwives. The poem was a breach birth. The poem forgot where it came from. Provenance was of no importance to the poem. The poem was panting in pentameter. The poem asked, What is the question? The poem was a miscellany of the absurd. The poem was always the same river. The poem was a panther beneath a rose tree. The poem was a naming ceremony. The poem made a necessary stain against the silence. The poem counted on more days of rain. The cockerel served as the poem's mascot, the young cock of the walk. The poem clapped a tambourine. The poem shattered a thousand glass tambourines. The poem was hot metal on an anvil prone. The poem was made whole through erasure. Some days the birds carried it to the poem. Some days, the poem caught it with a hook, like a fish. The poem had a laugher's high. The poem was a seminar. The poem was an adoring aubade. The poem was an arduous denouement. The poem made a blank page valuable by putting it into an exquisite frame. The poem was a blood disease. The poem was a lady in waiting. The poem was a gallant knight, born too late. The unwritten preface to the poem was: Here's my full thinking on the fallacy of love. The poem was a hundred years old when it went viral. The poem went viral when a beautiful young woman posted a video of herself reading it nude in a busy parking lot. The poem put to use the ampersand. The poem was not averse to ending a short list with etc. The poem detested people who were, objectively, detestable. The poem took a shortcut to a distant emotion. People talked about the poem, even when the poem was in the room. The big word had many syllables, but that didn't impress the poem. It was raining and then pouring and the poem was snoring. The poem was an admix of memory and desire. The poem was meant to be hollow, an empty vessel. The poem was thick with allusion. The poem was confused between one June and another September. The opening line of the poem was a popular tattoo among twenty-somethings. Sometimes there was a choir feeding lines to the poem. The poem elevated things of everyday use—the mixing bowl, the wheelbarrow, the family quilt. The poem was in portage, carrying a perilous canoe. Vanity, thy name is the poem. The poem italicized the word *forever* for several very good reasons. The poem had poetic license but not a valid driver's license. The poem had a hot take: perception is not reality. The poem thought, nothing is reality for very long. The poem was subsidized by a subsidizer. The poem was patronized by a patronizer. The poem was an eight-cylinder engine, a real gas-guzzler. The poem was a good haggler when it came to buying used cars. The poem was what the thunder said. The poem held hands with history. The poem's father was a greenskeeper at the local golf course, so there were always little pencils around the house. The poem gazed at its navel. The poem had canine intuition. The poem was a dirge dog. The poem was a shopping list for a fête. The poem was not a suicide note. The poem was scissors and paste. The poem was a recipe for delight. The poem was a résumé, a curriculum vitae. The poem was the sour note in a children's orchestra. The poem consulted a menu of options. The poem was a long list of terms and conditions. The poem reserved the right to be ever wrong. The poem was journalistic. The poem was visited by Doctor Who. The poem had baggage. The poem paused, a telling caesura. The poem was a queer hypothesis, a foundation of the gay science—the reasoning, logic, ethics, philosophy, and history of science. The poem's house was a decayed house. The poem featured five ancient allusions, and if the dear reader recognized just one, then the poem had hit its mark. The poem forecasted rains, long rains. The poem was an almanac of rain and ruin, of floods and landslides that caused electrical fires in canal towns. The poem had thick skin against social losses, but still hurt inside when recalling old slights. Each word in the poem was carefully chosen from a limitless vocabulary. The poem still had a few of its baby teeth. The poem resisted all forms of mothering. Finally published, the poem met its maker. The poem lived inside a cookie jar. The poem was a dull head among windy spaces. The poem spread cheese on a cracker, poured wine into a plastic glass. The poem sat cross-legged on the floor. The poem was an annuity. The poem had a very long tongue. The poem danced erect by the Nile. The poem was no more a city. The poem was dust. The poem was upbuilding. The poem let the sun shine in. The poem tickled the shy. The poem agreed with Belinda Carlisle—heaven is a place on earth. And the poem had one more thought about Belinda Carlisle—the life advice contained in the title of her fourth solo album, *Live Your Life Be Free*, was perhaps the greatest truth of all. The poem survived, at last count, three real-life O. Henry stories. The poem was stitched in needlepoint. The poem was animated, that is, drawn by an animator and brought to life in the animation studios of Walt Disney. The poem considered revision lapidary work. The poem rapped about the real world. The poem tried to put truth in a cage. The poem saved time in a bottle. The poem called attention to the fact that a politician who considered himself a strong man spoke almost entirely in sentences constructed in the passive voice. The poem said it was a good year for acorns, and so for squirrels. The poem was ever wishing to sunder things and things. The poem was careful in wishing and whiling. Rub-a-dub-dub, the poem was not alone in the tub. The poem watched the stars sink underwater. The poem had too many affectations to enumerate. The poem was naked on the page. The poem picked a daffodil, just one. The poem was nationalistic. The poem was unknown in her hometown. The poem had an audience among the illiterate. The poem was on fire. The poem poured forth speech. The poem reflected facts. The poem displayed knowledge. The poem waited for the day to end, an endurance test. The poem was a realist when it came to sex. The poem knew pestilence because the poem was a pest. The poem rolled to a stop without punctuation. The poem stiffened at the sight of cut flowers. The poem often failed for technical reasons. The poem tried to try again. The poem wanted more love and then another broken heart. The poem sang scat. The poem whistled perfectly. The poem renewed the alphabet, starting with the letter Aa. The poem clung to older canons. The poem was ever ripe. The poem heaped hyperbole upon metaphor. The poem was kindling for a fiery heart. The poem wore ridiculous beads. The poem was a traipser, directionless. The poem counted accents, not syllables. The poem had a logical texture. The poem looked like a monkey and smelled like one too. The poem was an impersonal pronoun. The poem was a person thanks to personification. It was through personification that the poem became God, creating man. The poem was a churching. The poem was about more than everybody else combined. The poem alternated lines of realism with lines of fancy. The poem played with pronouns. The poem played with her food to conceal an outsized appetite. The poem licked her thumb to turn another page in the dictionary, and what she tasted was words. The poem went to Paris between the wars in order to drink legally, and write freely—he called it exile and encouraged others to see it as exile, too. The poem was about a woman he thought he knew. The poem recalled the birth canal. The poem was a person, place, or thing. The poem was to, for, or about. The poem was a scaffolded experience pinned to a discredited personality test. There was another man within the poem who was very angry with him. The poem preferred vanilla to chocolate, and he was often forced to defend or apologize for this preference. The poem's t-shirt said, CRACK IS WHACK, but his feelings about crack were actually more nuanced than that. Life gave the poem lots of lemons. Yes, said the poem, I wear a bib. The poem was people from all walks of life. The poem was artifice but not artificial. The poem hid her feminine side. The poem still felt the OBGYN's forceps on her temples. The poem's dirty laundry accumulated on the floor of her bedroom in the form of a mandala. The poem was a gesture toward meaning. The poem was an endless string of worry beads. The poem had an uncompromising nature. The poem's theme song was "Little Miss Can't Be Wrong" by the band named Spin Doctors. The auctioneer told the poem he was going once…going twice…sold! The poem had a trident of charm, guts, and guile. After a brief refractory period, the poem was ready to go again. The poem was a hands-free selfie. Oftentimes, the poem was unreasonable for no good reason. The poem was a page and a half of neat tally marks. The poem was an action of the mind captured on a page. The poem ate men like air. The poem wasn't into poetry. The poem knew how to talk to angels. The poem had a superior air. The poem was an effervescent Virgo. The poem—who by all appearances was outgoing, loud even—was a soi-disant shy person. The poem loved peanut butter more and more each day. The poem's efforts to bulk up at the gym were not successful. The poem was a grudgey Taurus. The poem ate like a bird. The poem miscarried at thirteen weeks. The poem was missing a few teeth, which gave her a charming grin. The poem always had a little lisp-spittle on her chin. The poem squandered its existence for a pocketful of mumbles. The poem hunted similes to extinction. On a good day, the poem misfired on all cylinders. The poem didn't argue pronouns. The poem was seldom right and wrong again. The poem was a blinkered racehorse. The poem promoted a singular obliquity. A slight foxing of the pages in his first collection gave the poem an age-old elegance that beguiled serious bibliophiles. The poem felt sorry for herself all the time (she wasn't pretty, she wasn't smart, she wasn't good at *anything*), and she supposed everyone who knew her also felt sorry for her. The poem was a Gemini who adapted her dreams to suit an acceptable reality. The poem was a mind reader. The poem was an incomplete Enneagram. The poem put in order the ten minerals on Mohs hardness scale: talc, gypsum, calcite, fluorite, apatite, feldspar, quartz, topaz, corundum, and diamond. The poem was a girl with faraway eyes. When the poem used the word far, she meant never to be reached. The poem was a boy hunting for the first time. The poem was a spokesperson for the divine. The poem had two half-sisters. The poem left some blood behind on the page. The poem used the term ad hoc to mean half-assed. The poem made poetry out of poor prose. The poem had an abrupt page of thought, and then, all at once, the words began to run faster than he could write them down. The poem was pale for wariness of climbing heaven and gazing on the earth. The poem was a means of refuge from the miseries of life. At his day job, the poem did not mind getting reminders from colleagues about work that was due or nearly due. Like P. T. Barnum, the poem believed that every crowd had a silver lining. The poem lived in the house of his head. The poem was in communion with her childhood. The poem was a gymnast when she was a girl. With the advent of hip-hop, the poem became young again. The poem was loyal to his barber, his butcher, and several bartenders. The poem was not a pickup truck. The poem was not a station wagon or an SUV. The poem was not a sports car. The poem was a luxury sedan. The poem was a cellar dweller. The poem was sexually adventuresome. The poem was a cross between hopscotch and scotch on the rocks. The poem was a cross-threaded screw. The poem was a plumber's invective. The poem was a natural diuretic. The poem had a laxative quality. The poem was a royal flush. The poem listened for bagpipes when he broke the seal on a fresh bottle of single-malt. The poem was a flying-toaster screensaver. The poem knew the full extent of his ignorance. The poem blended nonsense with critical insights. The poem employed intuition to explore madness. The poem was a pocket veto. The poem had a wet voice. The poem was a soggy Pisces. The poem had a Cheshire cat frown. The poem enumerated the seven types of ambiguity: Sunday, Monday, Tuesday, Wednesday, Thursday, Friday, Saturday. The poem was superfluous but also somehow essential. The poem was a cat among pigeons. The poem moved from sight to recognition. The poem had babies, more words. The poem was a stillborn goat. The poem was everything, and then the poem was nothing. The poem was an untethered Aquarius. The poem guaranteed a viral moment. The poem was a horse-and-buggy poem, a charming conveyance. The poem was solitary, poor, nasty, brutish, and short. The poem was bigger than a breadbox. The poem kept time like a human beatbox. The poem was no heavier than an accordion. The poem had a premise and a purpose. The poem made emotions nebulous, she was a nebulizer. A spider appeared in the poem, so the poem became a spider poem. The poem found the true nature of the bonsai tree. The poem played one note, just one note in tune and on time. The poem had a forgiving vernacular. The poem was forward thinking and also froward thinking. The only accolades the poem received were mocking awards. The poem was actually an actuarial table printed in the 1950s. The poem had a self-effacing way when operating in a self-promotional mode. The poem was entering an enterprising phrase zone. The poem wished that there weren't so many other poems in the world. The poem was a wizard but didn't make a big deal about it. If the poem was trudging up a hill, the poem was tumbling down a hill. The poem possessed an echoing quiet. As a boy, the poem had an imaginary friend named Andy Hamburger who always came around during dinnertime. The poem was a discomposed neurotic mess. The poem had a shine. The poem had a sheen that was liquid in depth. The poem was within a finger's breadth of being mad. The poem was stiff as a board and light as a feather. Like a dog, the poem made sure to put a sniff on everything in its path. The poem was a promptly, not an eventually. The poem knew from furtive. The poem played the role of avuncular auntie in her extended chosen family. The poem was a classic Libra, often left behind, misplaced, overdrawn, melted. The poem was a clogged pore. The poem had flowering innards—she bloomed within. The poem had a corrupting effect on adolescents. The poem's own adolescence lasted for decades. The poem's specific gravity was immeasurable. In programming languages, the poem was a delimited continuation—a "slice" of a continuation frame that had been reified into a function, returning a value, and thus could be reused and composed to combine simple functions to build more complicated ones. The poem was mad and maddening to all who heard her fierce volubility. The poem mourned the life he never lived. When confronted by a broken-hearted former lover at the mall, the poem turned her pretty head and walked away. Years and years ago, the poem realized he was the black sheep of his family. The poem left her bed and wander'd alone, bareheaded, barefoot. The poem worked tirelessly to maintain his amateur status. The poem tried hard to be a slut, but it just wasn't in her. The poem wore an outrageous cape. The poem was more or less a toast to bygone days. The poem had many antennae. The poem was a hugger. The poem's signature animal was the possum. The poem couldn't abide by the rules of his family's trust. The poem was burned to the bone. The poem was a distraction, a misdirection to cover a sleight of hand. The poem was a love letter to Phoebe Bridgers. The wisdom of the poem fell on deaf eras. The poem was a member of the lost generation. The poem united a set of oppositions. Weak and weary, the poem pondered a midnight dreary. The poem was a looksee—a peek—at a part of the human body typically clothed. The poem was all genitals. The poem kissed a statue of the Virgin Mary in a church, and she became a virgin again. It was a beautiful evening, and the poem was calm and free. The poem was breathless with adoration. The poem contrasted the weight of a choice vs. that of a decision. Prone, the poem topped from the bottom. The poem made his own enemies. The poem tipped the scale at 103 lbs. The poem sought rhyme. The poem sought new structures to master and abandon. The poem sought no rewards. There was no envy in the poem—she lacked that bone. The poem wanted teetering in his life, sought imbalance, in fact. The poem sought new ways to hide his feelings, not express them. The poem sought agency. The poem sought a self beyond itself. The poem sought perfection. The poem desperately sought sleep. The poem sought an inescapable solitude. The poem sought perpetual change. The poem forgave itself when the perfection sought was not found. The poem sought a lot. The poem said what the poem said. The poem heard that an old colleague referred to him as a very nice man, and that pleased him. Through the ether, the poem heard the voice of Mahalia Jackson. As the poem grew old, he lost hair and gained weight, which was better than being dead. It was reported that the poem was the cardinal point in a bizarre love triangle, but, in truth, the poem was trapped inside an enigmatic love trapezoid. The poem was an inveterate anagrammer. The poem was a wound-licking surrender. There's a famous series of photos taken of the poem standing in front of a yellow 1969 Corvette Stingray. The poem was energized by the sight of young people. The poem took counsel from the hooded moon. The poem had a natural divinity. The poem was a confidant. The poem gave name to the parallelogram. The poem gave birth to the oblong. The poem found a path between originality and imitation. The poem adopted a new slang. The poem was happier with no mindset. The poem was growth, evolution, genesis. The poem penetrated the wall of failed explanations. Beyond self-care, the poem advocated strongly for self-preservation. The poem had a mellow fruitfulness. The poem lived in his head. The poem lived in thought. The poem lived in a townhouse far from any town. The poem was so lonesome, she could cry. The poem asked the fact for the form. The poem was a tie-dyed t-shirt with a steal-your-face logo. The poem was alive today and it was always today. The poem was in praise of all that deserved praise. Counting aloud, the poem buckled his shoes, shut the door, and picked up sticks. The poem was precocious well into his forties. In his first-grade classroom, the poem was made to stand at the chalkboard beneath the letter Tt because he caused so much trouble. The poem was in dry dock all season. The poem was locked into a generative mode. The poem had a personality founded on the paraphernalic regalia of the Boston Celtics. The poem put on its editor's cap. The poem was never comfortable in academic regalia. The poem was pregnant and it was Halloween, so she went to the costume party as a pregnant nun. The poem was a strobe light. The poem was a disco ball. The poem was a laser light show in the planetarium. The poem had fallen low. The poem put scare quotes to purpose the way a farmer puts a scarecrow to work in his cornfield. The poem was a convocation. The poem was a cavalcade. The poem was the fattest baby ever born at the small hospital in her hometown, and the newspaper ran a photo of her under an all-caps headline, JANUARY JUMBO TIPS SCALE AT 13 LBS. 8 OZ! The poem was a commencement. The poem argued that the hokey-pokey was about a hell of a lot more than putting your left foot in and shaking it all about, then putting your right foot in and shaking it all about. The poem's resting heartbeat was love. The poem had one good eye. The poem, in forced exile, wrote of his homeland with affection. The poem had baby-bearing hips but not a child-rearing head. It was all mumbo-jumbo, but the poem's mumbo-jumbo was core to its aesthetic. The board of education deemed the poem masturbatory. The poem concerned a miscarriage. The poem gained power through memorization. The poem was stored in so many heads. The poem, originally read as an apologia, was literally a corrective. The poem was young, intelligent, and slightly drunk. The poem was loathe to use the word lacuna, but this is what was killing him. The poem was a natural falsetto. The poem said, That's my soul up there. The poem was out of compass, but not off course. The poem had a leaping mind. Caslon, Garamond, Janson, not just fonts but saints to the poem. The poem was in command at all times. The poem was a pollinator. The poem was a homily. The poem was a sensory event. The poem removed all impediments to God. The poem was a prayer. The poem was a votive lit. The poem knew what the ostrich saw in the sand. Critics spoke of the poem's scaffolding. To call the poem cosmic, does that elevate it? The poem did not want to be praised. The poem did not want to be understood. The poem wanted to be read, simply read. The poem was ten days late, but she knew she wasn't pregnant. The poem courted fandom. The poem savored the radical devotion of his followers. The poem silenced many. The poem had a younger sister, named Melody, whom he teasingly called Malady. The poem did a terrible job at marketing itself. The poem asked, Who goes there? The poem craved attention. The poem thought every baby picture he saw was him when he was a baby. The poem vocalized, and not just in words. The poem gossiped. The poem was a refuser. The poem yearned to be kindly. The poem observed that the Pandemic accelerated his aging process and his wife's, but it had the opposite effect on their four children, whose maturation was regressively disrupted, delayed. The poem died in paraphrase and explication. The poem looked good in her new jeep. The poem was a combination lock. The poem thrived in marginalia. The poem was about sex and death. Like a loaf of bread, the poem was doughy and crusty. The poem tripped upon synecdoche. The poem popped upon onomatopoeia. The poem made an ass out of assonance. The poem was stuck in a long line at the Starbucks drive thru. The poem grew up to become a soccer mom. The poem wore a wax mask, pretending to be a candle. The poem functioned in the blood like insulin. The poem was an object lesson but for whom? The poem spoke into a microphone. In his last phase, the poem grew gnomic. The poem didn't give a fart—check that—the poem didn't give a *farthing* about anybody but himself. The poem was a plot of one thousand acres where memories grew. The boulevard was full of the poem's footsteps—he had not disappeared. The poem reeked of misfortune. The poem drowned in a steamer trunk, crossing the Atlantic. The poem disseminated misinformation. The poem was written in lowercase, after cummings. The poem was guilty as a bug. The poem was making like a rug. Everybody walked all over the poem. The poem, like the sea lark, twittered sweetly. The poem was exercising regularly and feeling trim. The poem likened her personality to lichen. The poem was menstruating. The poem was an unstitched wound. The poem burned away all the peripherals. The poem was a poem even in prose. The poem pointed at frauds. The poem started arguments. The poem took sides. The poem tried to stop the world from going to sleep. The poem was composed of a couple dozen couplets. When the poem was a child, his mother tried, but failed, to get an ADHD diagnosis for him. The poem was nonsensical, but it was not nonsense. The poem was whimsical because it had quite a lot of whimsy in its bones. The poem's portrait had been painted many a time. The poem was an anthem to the power ballad. The poem was the closing moments of a rock opera. The poem was as precise as geometry. The poem was produced through the hard manual labor of imagination. The poem would not be ignored. The poem came from hunger. The poem was hungry. The poem cleaned up our word-clogged reality by creating silences around things. The poem braided her hair too tight. The poem felt a kinship with October—co-opted with its Rocktober radio marketing assaults and its Socktober fundraising campaigns. The poem was limber as a ghost. The poem conducted an orchestra of birds. In deep sleep, the poem snored. The poem slept in the buff, and so she was naked in all of her dreams. The poem dropped one or two feathers in the field. Word on the street was the poem was down to fuck. The poem knew the rules to many card games: gin, rummy 500, tripoley, scat, spit, spoon, euchre, hearts, spades, pitch, pinochle, five-card stud, Texas hold 'em (which he called Texas fold 'em), blackjack, Omaha hi-lo 8, razz, to name but a few. In the seventies, the poem had what was called at the time an identity crisis. The poem's menstrual cycle was like a run-on sentence—she never knew when her periods would end. The poem's menstrual cycle was continuous. The poem plucked out a four-note tune on her lyre. The poem tickled the ivories. The poem pumped a pump organ. The poem squeezed a squeezebox. The poem blew softly on an aeolian harp. The poem couldn't recall how she came to own a ukulele. The poem had a few dull tattoos, nothing worth showing off. No ink was wasted on the poem's body. The poem ascribed to the show-don't-tell school of writing. The poem loved rock 'n' roll, so she put another dime in the jukebox. The poem was a bare lightbulb, hot and bright. The poem was a light anchor, but it was heavy enough to still a tiny boat. Nonetheless was the poem's go-to position. The poem rebranded Never-never Land as Nevertheless Land. The poem gave away too much of himself. The poem had to be taught how to save the best of himself for himself. The poem was more powerful than government-made adrenochrome. The poem pointed at people even though it was impolite to point. The poem was nursing a secret crush on another poem. The poem collected disparities, non sequiturs. The poem had an inner-ear infection that brought on aural hallucinations. The poem remembered everything, even that which she longed to forget. The poem wore a peplum top that flattered her figure. The poem lived inside a nativity scene snow globe. The poem was not acquisitive. The poem was a bricolage. Women followed the poem wherever he went. The poem was devastating in heels, but she mostly wore flats. The poem rode high on a penny-farthing, peddling his ass off. The poem prized his innocence. The poem left room for dessert. The poem took questions after her reading. The poem was undocumented. The poem was deported. The poem was a passport. The poem found, by his unbelief, a life of doubt diversified by faith and a life of faith diversified by doubt. The poem was a limited liability company, which gave him protection against a raft of lawsuits. The poem was bald and wild as Britney Spears in the summer of 2007. On most subjects, the poem said the opposite of what she really thought so as not to cause offense. The poem was the last of the true believers. Whereas, the poem began and then promptly stopped. The poem was a wart on a witch's chin. The poem was vacuous. The poem had a half-life comparable to that of plutonium. Halfway holy was the poem. The poem served fish to countless apostles. The poem was a Scorpio who could not control her venom. The poem had money in the bank. The poem had assets. The poem had debts. The poem had a balanced checkbook. There was screaming in the poem's head—its volume was low, as if heard from a distance. The poem was reminded to vary expression from one line to the next. The poem didn't know its boundaries. The poem was denominated in the inflated currency of irony. Bad news always seemed to reach the poem on her cell phone, so her relationship with her cell phone became fraught. The poem ignored most people because most people ignored the poem. The poem was luckless but not charmless. The poem would never die because it was too important. The poem feared the madness in all things. There is no waste with piranhas, the poem observed. The poem seemed light as a shallow river flowing over sandy beaches. The poem was like the duck gently gliding across a still pond, paddling furiously below the surface. The poem was simply the most beautiful, impressive, and widely effective mode of saying things, hence its importance. The poem mixed abstraction with the concrete. The poem fettered the human race. The poem was an invisible priest. The poem drank heartily from a bulging wineskin. The poem played bass in a traditional Irish band called the Willin'

Fools. The poem used clouds as a verb. The poem's adjective game was on point, virtually unassailable. The poem rehabilitated the adverb, slowly, to avoid detection. The poem was the Q-text for the synoptic gospels of Matthew, Mark, and Luke. At bottom, the poem was a criticism of life. The poem loaded every rift with ore. Physically, the poem felt as if the top of her head had been taken off. The poem was immodest. The poem dropped a rose petal down the Grand Canyon and waited for an echo. The poem was a hierophant. The poem was a legislator. The poem experienced the horrors of sordid passion. The poem's spirit was a flimsy curtain swept this way and that by the slightest breeze. The poem was sometimes consumeful and sometimes produceful. The poem wore a black leather biker jacket when she was out on the prowl. God spoke the poem's name. God gave life to the poem. The poem was born in a godforsaken country and died there, too. The poem never learned to swim. The poem was a bad little actress. The poem fought back tears. There were little tears in the fabric of the poem's soul. The poem was a lot of people's Wonderwall. The poem's heart was like a wheel. The poem had a hunger to be, to always be. The poem had a thirst to be on tongues and lips, to be bitten by white teeth. The poem leapt beyond existence. The poem was a glory stream from heaven above. The poem was a webinar. The poem asked, Why did Eve fuck Satan? The poem was particles, waves. The poem had a cowardly imagination. The poem was an anchor in the drift of the world. The poem was a widower of what. The poem named its loss Daisy, because daisies were everywhere. The poem wore a little black dress. The poem had no sense of personal space. The poem was either a dog in one of its recent past lives or would be born a dog in the next. The poem was struck by lightning more than a dozen times. The poem had some chestnuts squirreled away in an old notebook. The poem was written in response to an urgent blind prompt designed to break everyday, garden-variety writer's block. The poem was an acne scar, wide as an inground pool. The poem was a UFO spotted by a few farmers tending their fields. The poem was a set of illegible crop circles. The poem was not about its rhyme scheme. The poem was too tall. The poem was an ATM of imagery. The poem was adored because the poem was adorable. The poem had an irregular sleep pattern. The poem carved heads on cherry-stones. A critic called the poem pointless, and the poem told the critic, I am not pointless, sir, but I am useless. Air traffic controllers frequently reported the poem as in anomalous blip on their busy radar screens. The poem pondered immensements. The poem would cut off an ear if that hadn't already been done to death. The poem was a macaroon, a spinning top, a snow sled. The poem gave blood at the Red Cross pop-up donation center. The poem was a Martian to many. The poem preferred to play tennis with the nets down. The poem was at home with her tits out and a book and a drink. The poem thrived among his fellow communards. The poem asked its reader to make a choice between vulgarity and banality. The poem started raining and never stopped. The poem invented the wheel, set it rolling. The poem was an imperceptible lodestar. The poem was a forgotten landmark. The poem was a lodestone that had lost its magnetism. The poem was a compass rose. The poem heard tubular bells. The poem was a renunciation of The Annunciation. The poem had one inverted nipple, which seemed a metaphor. Sometimes the poem forgot what she was bitching about. The poem was hard to live with, she knew. The poem was peopled with lovers struggling with love, artists struggling with art, drinkers struggling with drink. The poem was a grift. The poem was a paraliterary parasite. The poem was a death-row harmonica solo. The poem was the titular neighbor with the dirty knees. The poem was a drug snuggler—not a drug smuggler, a drug snuggler. The poem cleaned its ear with a toothpick. The poem was a sadsack. The poem was puppies, kittens, chickadees. The poem was guppies. The poem was the first person. The poem was the second person. The poem was the third person. Like Picasso, the poem captured its subjects from multiple points of view at once. The poem had groupies that followed him from city to city. The poem was dogmatic as a metronome. The poem scaled tall buildings. The poem moved mountains. The poem smelled of toupee glue at the discotheque. The poem wasn't like other poems. The poem was a well-attended orgy. A thick coating of vernix encased the poem prenatally. The poem was kinda sorta in love again. The poem was marred by its liberal use of etc. The poem was a 3-D printer. Yes, the poem's heart flipped a beat at the sight of the woman he would later come to marry. The poem sold sanctuary in the form of soulful trinkets. The poem sold fertilizer for the soul. The poem liked to begin the day donning a mask and peering into a mirror. The poem skipped a flat rock across a still pond. The poem was about a day in the life of a Beatle. The poem had dizzy spells that often lasted for weeks. The poem was diagnosed with dizzy-lady syndrome. The poem had come upon another reckoning. The poem felt strongly that she had to live up to the aspirations, the profundity of her title. Safe in the beehive, loaded with honey, the poem served his queen. The poem said, Those Kennedy boys were good for catching the clap and catching bullets. The poem was an acrostic that longed to be an abecedarium, as all poems do. The poem was also a telestich, though few looked closely enough to notice. The poem was meant to be a gateway drug for young readers unaware of the addictive properties of poesy. The poem was a baby rattle and a death rattle. The poem wept. The poem swept. The poem crept. The poem slept. The poem leapt to easily drawn conclusions that also served as effective endlines. The poem was adept at childlike wordplay. The poem kept an exhaustively faithful dream diary. The poem learned to accept that he was the exception that proved the rule of threes. The poem's whole life was contained the first chapter of *Little Women*, that is, a dreadful, poor

Christmas. The poem discovered naturally occurring train tracks deep in the woods. The poem saw the light at the end of the tunnel, and it portended an oncoming train. The poem had the ability to ferment any liquid, making potent potables. The poem felt a loneliness that wasn't his. The poem had a tongue of flame, an arm extended burning. The poem licked a sugar cube. The poem sugared the pill. The poem had some outstanding IOUs. The poem got about on crutches. The poem didn't belong to anyone, and nothing belonged to the poem. The poem had a simple psychology. The poem's head was screwed on straight. Every time he left the house, the poem's mother said, They're all gonna laugh at you. The poem recalled the time when first she practiced to deceive. The poem knew how to clear a room with just a few recited lines of Donne. The flea and the poem mingled the blood of two. The poem was 86'd from a favorite dive. The poem was an overachieving Aries. The poem heard a song high above the trees. The poem had a voice as big as the sea. The poem wasn't a total fuck up, but he fucked up a lot. The poem policed his bad intentions. Virtually all of the poem's crimes went undetected. The poem was a smooth criminal. The poem investigated the dark portion of his psyche. The poem was prosecuted for a seriously bad pun. The poem began as a pensum. The poem was imprisoned at a minimum-security facility—located on the moon of course! The poem was labeled a docupoem, and she liked that label. The poem's shadow was trying to thwart him. The poem always wore black because he was in mourning for his own life. If she was allowed to wear rubber gloves, the poem was willing to touch anything. The poem was stripped of her robe by a pair of clever schoolboys and left to stand naked in a fetid middle school classroom. The poem got real. The poem got into some real talk. The poem was a crumbling grey stone wall. The poem was an uneven, rangy privet. The poem was a thicket. The poem was a good kisser, everyone said. The poem was in love again, and he love love loved it. The poem made a note to google if Bobby Short ever met Wayne Shorter—perhaps they collaborated. The poem was the sum of its swanky style points. The poem was shallow but made up for its lack of depth with a vast surface area. The sun knew the poem. The poem got a sunburn, then freckled. The poem was asleep but soon would wake. The poem made threats and kept promises. Maybe the poem had an extra chamber in his heart, pumping out all that lovey-dovey bullshit. The poem had many hobbies. The poem was an inveterate hobbyist. The poem courted bad habits. What were once vices had become habits for the poem. The horses are on the track, said the poem. The poem played the ponies. The poem placed bets on fast horses ridden by very small men. The poem made anagrams of the names of the horses in the last race of the day, but he did not place a bet. The poem made no vows, but pursued an avocation. The poem made a career of play. The poem occasionally risked absurdity. The poem was a full-time job. The poem was in hibernation. The poem had seasonal affective disorder. The poem was never more than peripheral. The poem exposed his limitations with the language. The poem was reasonably pleased with the quality of his recent erections. The poem was made of his savior. The poem was quiet with the O-gape of complete despair. Some put on a high-mannered voice when they read the poem aloud. Some readers heard a different voice in their head when they read the poem to themselves. At the gym, the poem exercised her imagination in a racy spin class. After his workout, the poem lingered in the sauna, sweating gin and vermouth. The poem hung her laundry on the clothesline to dry in the dirty breeze. The poem was untitled. There was a reason the poem was untitled, but that reason is now unremembered. The poem originally titled "Untitled" was written by a poet who nobody remembers. The poem "Untitled" was titled "Untitled." That is, the poem was given a title and then the given title was taken back? The poem untitled was a prank. The poem untitled was the bride stripped bare. The reasons to title the poem untitled were many—boorishness, cheekiness, contemptuousness, dickishness, glibbishness, laziness, loutishness, pithiness, superciliousness, superficialness, wiliness, worthlessness, youthfulness, to name but a few. A poem titled "Untitled" had no fitness, the poem believed. If a poem's title was meant to be read as the first line of the poem, then what kind of a poem was a poem titled "Untitled?" All poems titled "Untitled" have a bit of an entitled attitude that rubs a majority of readers the wrong way. The poem knew of several poems that carried an even more shameful title: "Untitled, II." Scholars and critics often gave the poem's untitled poems titles for the sake of disambiguation. The poem "Untitled" written by a poet named Anonymous—that's a nothing burger. The poem titled "Untitled" stood as a big fuck you to every titled poem. A poem's title is its promise, the poem believed. Being untitled, the poem lived a life without dignity. The poem busted through an old picket fence and served Kool-Aid on the other side. The poem explored the nebulous galaxy. The poem was out of quarters and the arcade fell silent to his ears. The poem had a silence all its own. The poem delineated a path for the soul to follow. The poem was a pioneer who walked backwards. The poem committed an epistolary infidelity. The poem was a bee tasting the spring. The poem was the irrelevant parent in the house. The poem went to college with a girl named Sylvia Plaid. The poem was worse than the truth. The poem was an erased de Kooning. After decades of neglect, the poem was being read again. The poem thrived among fellow communards. In quarantine, the poem grew odder and odder still. The poem was adorned with adjectives. The poem measured the distance between her teardrops. The poem was living on reds, vitamin C, and cocaine. After thirty, the poem woke up sad every morning. The poem suffered from chinlessness. The poem was an irritant lazily making a pearl. The poem defined running as a method of terrestrial locomotion by which humans and other animals move rapidly on foot. An invasive survey, the poem was called. The poem was a menacing busker, strumming hard and singing at the top of his voice. The poem possessed an alien set of values. The poem was a sexist surmise. The poem played the sousaphone. The poem was a face-melting guitar solo. The poem was a riddling paradiddle. The poem tooted its own horn. The poem had many natural adornments. The poem was decorated with life. Butter wouldn't melt in the poem's mouth. The poem was a circus in climax. The poem was a miniature minotaur moving his house. The poem's first green was gold. The poem was hopeless. The poem laid a road for the bold to follow. The poem transmitted dance to words. Upon an unseen grid, the poem danced. The poem was the face of herself when she was young. Dubbed a dummy, the poem played the diswitted simpleton. The poem sought stillness in body and thought. The poem was a body unblemished by sin. The poem was a semaphore. The poem was a lighthouse. The poem was a foghorn. The poem was a warning shot. The poem was a shag-golfer calling out, Fore! The poem was a ghost living in a synthesizer. The poem had something for everybody. The poem was an organism of delight and pity. The poem was a loose queue that could straighten itself with some prompting. The poem was written speech to text and read text to speech. The poem existed on the page and on the tongue and in the ear. The poem existed outside of realism and was therefore able to reveal deeper human truths. The poem dreamed in exposition. The poem identified the dominant odor in every church and house of worship: denture adhesive. The poem was a primitive artificial intelligence that applied characteristics such as word frequencies and collocations procreatively. The poem was God manifest in the mind. The poem was a yellowing moon on the wane. The poem was a rhythm attached to a rhyme. The poem was distant. The poem was a rupture. The poem was waiting for trouble, not hiding from it, just waiting for trouble to find her. The poem wore unflattering clothes because it was the only way she could get through the day without being hit on by every man who crossed her path. The poem's nuclear option was activated by the delete key. The poem was an example of a healthy psychological transference. The poem read bad books fast and good books slowly. The poem used to time herself doing the word search puzzles in the Sunday papers. The poem relied on its readers' regnant belief in a higher being, a creator. The poem was like a cheeky ghost, using *boo* in lieu of punctuation. The poem took a quick power nap and was ready for the world. The poem was a multiverse of incongruity and conflicting narratives that all led to the same inexorable outcome. The poem was a good guy who always won. The poem was a loser who stopped trying to win. There was some heat around the poem again, after a rapper quoted a few of its lines. The poem was a death document. The poem unsleeved the crackers, cut the cheese, uncorked the wine. The poem strained to play the role of hostess. The poem said, with some certainty, There's only one career path in the afterlife. The poem was neither a gentleman nor a scallop. The poem was a shot in the dark. The poem was a lark's tongue in aspic. The poem was not a quitter. The poem was the opposite of a quitter. The poem was a fighter. The poem accepted that the world was round but not that it was spinning. As his wife began her menopause, the poem began to experience something like a second puberty. The poem felt that adults who did not have children remained children in observably childish ways. There was an unnaturalness about the poem—an almost alien quality. The poem was not a philosophy. The poem was a refutation of philosophy. The poem ironed out the folds of her inner ear, so she could hear her inner voice more clearly. In support of the serial comma, the poem used multiple commas between each item in a list. These multiple commas had the surreal appearance of a dripping ellipsis, thought the poem. The poem played up her secondary sexual characteristics. The poem wore bright red lipstick, blue eyeshadow, thick mascara, false eyelashes. The poem was always in a hurry. In haste, the poem made waste. Charm was a quality that the poem had in abundance. Said another way, The poem had an assload of fucking charm. The poem was incapable of change but not averse to revision. The poem often left an exposed revision in a final draft. The poem was quick to congratulate himself on precise word choice. The poem dispelled myths. The poem often misspelled the names of mythological characters. The poem was a domesticated dragon that exhaled smoke but produced no fire. The poem told the wall to meet her at the corner. Dippin' Dots, the poem mused, had been calling itself the Ice Cream of the Future ever since she was a little girl. The poem had only one rule to live by—always be yourself. The poem always put in her best effort because effort is the only thing that anyone can really control in life. The poem believed foundationally that all things must be kept in moderation. The poem definitely had a favorite Beatle, and his name was George Harrison. The poem had a trite streak that ran counter to her best instincts. The poem warned others not to tether themselves to outmoded systems of behavior. The poem believed that fat people should not be allowed to wear sneakers. The poem wanted more of the same. The poem interviewed a new assistant. The poem would do anything to hit a higher note. The poem was in a self-induced coma. The poem was acquainted with the night, and longed to know it intimately. The poem was a frolic. The poem was a non-alcoholic beer. The poem was an effective lesson in flirtatious winking. The poem went through a witchy period that amounted to two lengthy stanzas of black magic and demon summoning. The poem collected broken clocks—actually fixed a few. The poem was an out-of-the-box solution. The poem had reach and reputation. The poem came from the region on the map that was labelled, Here Be Dragons. The poem was a pusher. The poem was proof of the pathetic fallacy. The poem was chocolatey good. The poem was a gurgling stream. The poem was a babbling brook. The poem was a bubbling water fountain. The poem was a shallow lake, a muddy pond, a slow-rolling river, a roaring ocean. The poem was stuck in load mode, bogged down in buffering. Fertility was no concern for the poem. The poem's alcohol intake was totally out of hand. The poem was still a primitive formation. The poem wasn't perfect. The poem was a loaded gun. The poem had an itchy hair-trigger finger. The poem wanted to shoot. The poem took a very long time in aiming. The poem stretched the truth a bit and a bit and a bit. The poem became comfortable with lies. What the poem constructed was a lattice of lies. The poem was never at a loss for words. Constrained was a feeling foreign to the poem. The poem was seriously bent on saving souls. The poem was kinky in ways that her lovers didn't notice. The poem paid the annual excise tax. The poem was tasked with producing a taxonomy of poets, by kingdom, phylum, class, order, family, genus, species. The poem had two sets of eyes. The poem saw everything. The poem sang "Suddenly Seymour," and she meant every word. The poem woke up every morning with a smile on her face to show the world all the love in her heart. The poem wrote yet another one about a man who wasn't good enough for her. The poem waltzed the aisles of the Five & Dime. The poem knew of a miner who died from miner's lung. The poem knew of a baker who died from baker's lung. When the poem thought about the miner and the baker, he became short of breath. The poem came to understand that marriage vows don't mean very much at all. Tinnitus sufferers found relief in reading the poem. The poem was cinematic, projecting vast landscapes, endless horizons. The poem's face was like something out of Hollywood's Golden Era, with cheekbones for days, kissably plump lips, and eyes lit from within. The poem was a drug that extended a feeling of wistfulness. The poem was heir to a throne somewhere. The poem said, We need a national holiday—nay, a worldwide holiday—to celebrate our coordinating conjunctions. The poem reserved the right to wrap itself in paradox for protective purposes. The poem had a multitude of self-protective guises. The poem was an exfoliant. The poem was a depilatory. The poem boasted of many charming assets, none of which were visible. The poem wheatpasted broadsides on the castle walls. The poem did not forget the thorns. The poem had a thorny memory. As soon as the poem stopped rolling, it started to gather moss. When the poem fell off her vigorous exercise regime, she gathered mass…in her ass. The poem took a fierce moral inventory, searching for the roots of her addiction. The poem's self-examination contained two lies, but they were dearly held lies. Once, when playing two truths and a lie, the poem offered three lies. The poem declined to play truth or dare because there was no such thing as truth, and because life itself was daring enough without doing something foolish. The poem found work selling souvenirs at a seaside shoppe. The poem generated mental energy from the alphabet like a windmill converts the breeze to electricity. This business about the moon, the poem said it is a thing of ours—the moon is there for all of us to call our own. If the poem were a woman, he could claim more of the moon, its cycle, its pull, its generous fertility, its succour. The poem mastered the art of losing. There was no doubting the poem's virtue. The poem was often recited at weddings. The poem woke early, greeted the dawn knowing that the rest of the day was going to be all motherfuckers, just motherfucker after motherfucker with no let up. The poem owed April an apology. The poem's favorite month was *not* June. Asked to name his favorite month, the poem replied, Maybe May. The poem was forever feathering her nest with kill fees for her blackmail poems. The poem hinged on false context and mistaken identity. The poem was completely operational and all of its circuits were functioning perfectly. The poem's senses were working overtime. The poem was like a self-basting turkey—or a Sunday pot roast stewing in its own juices. The poem had a lump in his throat for two decades, and those were glorious years. The poem was a charming little psychopath. The poem took a swan dive into the shallow end of his family's gene pool. The poem fed lies to his family. Like new legislation, the poem was a guardrail for safety against power. The poem dated a sweet socialist and then a cute communist and then a darling democrat and finally a rough-and-ready republican. The poem was non-denominational. The poem was apolitical. The poem's vote could be bought. The poem knew it was a honey trap, but he *loved* honey. The poem confessed to impure thoughts, and the priest behind the screen gasped. The poem could not access the Human Resources portal because the poem was neither human nor resourceful. The poem knew a sex swing when she saw one. The jury was still out on the poem's fate. The poem had quite a lot of effing and jeffing in it. The poem inherited a gold bar that was the size and shape of an iPhone. Imagine the poem in neon, flashing bright and true. The poem was high and bright and doing just fine, with a large ice coffee and a straw to drink it. The poem's testicles were muy grande. The poem's testicles were like fists. The poem's hair was all bristly, matted thistles, moldy straw. The poem was bound by no injunctions. The poem was a capricious Capricorn. The poem searched for its accurate self. The poem was a tally of deprivations. The poem turned water into wine, lead into gold, cliché into proverb. The poem blew out all but one of the candles on her birthday cake. The poem lived in a quiet small house in the country. No, the poem had no home. The poem identified as a cisgender male until they didn't. The poem was asexual. Hirsute, the poem was not. None of her lovers believed her when she told them, but pubic hair never appeared on the poem—her legs and underarms were naturally hairless as well. The poem wrote a series of systems poems. The poem was flying low—he had failed to zip up his pants again. Goddess was the only adjective that captured the poem in whole. The poem was an over-promising under-delivering Sagittarius. As a kid, the poem slept under his bed most nights. The poem recalled kindnesses. There had only been a few kindnesses in the poem's life. The poem sent greeting cards to loved ones, strangers, celebrities. The poem was like a funk band with a poor rhythm section. The poem was cross pollinated with a drawing-room drama, the result was a text that could be read as an effective douche or a so-so enema. The poem was a fast-acting and long-lasting mouthwash. The poem became less voluble after she quit smoking. The poem was an ode to the old days. Some lines in the poem were composed with predictive text. The poem didn't appreciate sarcasm. Sincerity was the poem's default mode. The poem imagined a character and then wrote a series of statements from the point of view of the character that made a case for forgiveness. Inch by inch, row by row, the poem made her garden grow. The poem spanked the maid, then read his morning newspaper, drinking a cup of weak tea. The poem got used to being looked at through the lenses of others. The poem suffered lifelong from prose dysmorphia. The poem's muscle for prosody had atrophied. The poem was an old-fashioned girl and so was her bosom. The poem's philanthropy was modest but consistent, making gifts annually (loyally) to a local hospital, his three favorite museums, his undergraduate college and graduate school, PETA, the World Wildlife Foundation, the March of Dimes, to name but a few. The poem was a party crasher. The world was too much with the poem. The poem was a parable. The poem was a morality play. The poem ate myth. The poem was living in a minor key. The poem was sufficient. The poem was a purgative. The poem worshipped warships. The poem was a sad little boy riding a hand-me-down girl's bike. The poem put on a pointy party hat and did his best to smile. The poem was pretty when she cried. The poem was exquisitely inquisitive. The poem was like a deep mine that could not be depleted. The poem was a little teapot, short and stout. The poem was a fertile turtle, productive, but slow. The poem was one of those aunties who are best described as avuncular. The poem was bluer than blue, sadder than sad. The poem crashed a golf cart at his grandmother's retirement village. The poem came from a country where all the men looked exactly the same— black eyes, black hair, foolish black mustaches. The poem had too much time to write, too much time to think. The poem was reckless. The poem never went through an awkward phase. The poem was at a loss for words. The poem failed a field sobriety test. The poem summoned itself. The poem appeared. The poem was constituted on the page. The poem evolved. The poem was fruitful. The poem multiplied. The poem was multiplicative. The poem was at the center of all beauty. The poem was an outsider. The poem was a grand opening, an unveiling, a ribbon-cutting. The poem lit a sensory constellation. The poem was an activist because it had a point of view. The poem had the biggest eyes and the wildest ears. The poem was known to wander lonely as a cloud. The poem promised perfection. The poem was an unexpected lunar eclipse. The poem was born a contravener. The poem had the body odor of four men—it was famously strong. The poem portrayed itself perfectly in all public appearances. The poem was an act of folly. The poem was an act of betrayal. The poem was an act of contrition. The poem was an act of desperation. The poem was an act of defilement. The poem was an act of homage. The poem said, Believe me. The poem was a binding contract. The poem was a paean. The poem was safe in a baby carriage. The poem was justice deferred. The poem said, Let's pretend to be friends. The poem was a neighbor's dog barking all night long. The poem established that roses are red and violets are blue; from those inarguable truths, the poem could begin to prove anything in a rhyme. The poem picked daisies on the side of a quiet freeway at dawn. The poem was deflowered in her aunt's basement. The poem was written a few miles above Tintern Abbey in a hot air balloon. The poem foretold of a struggle that would occupy mankind for many generations to come. The poem was a woman tied to the railroad tracks, but there was no train in sight. The poem was a heated swimming pool filled with beautiful young skinny-dippers. The poem summarized itself—a perfect precis with no extraneous words. The poem's favorite mnemonic was Please Excuse My Dear Aunt Sally, not only because it helped him to remember the algebraic order of operations (Parenthesis, Exponents, Multiply, Divide, Add, Subtract), but because he had an aunt named Sally, and his dear Aunt Sally was known to say semi-offensive things that she begged others to excuse. The poem wanted to be alone, which was not easy to achieve. The poem was a marathon, not a sprint. The poem was a sonnet without conflict and therefore impotent. The poem quarreled with the laws of inertia. The poem was a 1968 Ford Mustang convertible. The poem was a 1952 Studebaker coupe. The poem had four wheels on the ground and one in the trunk, a spare. The poem was a loveseat, two cushions smothered in fat fanny pheromones. The poem was an imitation of life. The poem was an intimation at intimacy. The poem was an inmate in a minimum-security prison. The poem cast a crippling shadow on a generation of poets. The poem was more of a marinade than a condiment. The poem was a spotlight-seeking Leo. The poem was the fiery index to the genius of the age. The poem was a mystery dishonestly marketed as a thriller. The poem was an almanac, trusty in regards to long-range weather forecast for crop management and up-building axioms to combat the symptoms of lonely farmer syndrome. The poem pulled into Nazareth, feelin' about half-past dead. The poem needed someplace to lay his head. The poem was several acronyms. The poem was attacked by a gang of antonyms. The poem was rescued by an agency of synonyms. Speaking of agency, the poem granted it freely to her readers. The poem made a list of retronyms: acoustic guitar, manual typewriter, analog watch, silent film, to name but a few. The poem was a rusty catheter. The poem had a few bad habits that he could not shake. Whenever the poem made new friends, she would absorb their good habits— e.g., exercise, hydration, skincare—into her daily routine. The poem went from station to station. The poem was a noiseless, patient spider. The poem was a spider from Mars. The poem had drops of Jupiter in her hair. The opening words of the poem were like the blank leader on a cassette tape that had no music but was designed for the purpose of cleaning the tape-heads before the music played. The poem had the wrong words in the wrong order. The poem was like the air in Dizzy Gillespie's big frog cheeks, a part of the instrument as much as the upturned trumpet. The poem was Satan in the bud. The poem had a daily tai chi practice that buoyed him through life's travails. The poem was not an apologia. The poem was too good to be true. The poem was a woman who had been taught to hold her tongue. The poem was a curse at first and then a sworn promise. The poem was neither fish nor fowl. The poem's academic itinerancy defined her life. The poem stared a hole through the back of the head of the poem sitting at one of the desks in the front row of the classroom. The poem aimed to be Emerson's transparent eyeball. At the stoplight, the poem studied his reflection in the rearview mirror. The poem masturbated to the ladies underwear pages of JC Penney catalogue. The poem masturbated to the ladies underwear pages of the Sears catalogue. The poem masturbated to every page of the Victoria's Secret catalogue. The poem masturbated to a pile of *Playboy* magazines he found in the woods. The poem masturbated to vintage 1970s pornography. The poem enumerated the dimples on a golf ball. The poem had a tele-therapy appointment at 7:00 a.m. every Thursday. The poem had a little overbite that telegraphed her smiles. The poem had entered the ducks-donkeys-dicks phase of his life. The poem tried to type, sucks-donkey-dick, but autocorrect took over the composition. The poem was a cashier's check. The poem was an invoice. The poem rowed its boat gently down the stream. The poem brought the conversation back to the moon. Like a cat, the poem had admiration, endless sleep, and company only when she wanted it. The poem was a connoisseur of comfort. The poem made way for ugly ducklings. The poem had no sense of humor. In a simple turn, the poem's face went from Melpomene to Thalia. Quoting her mother, the poem said, We don't fuck the face. The poem was researching laser tattoo removal, revising her body of work. The poem was an oath filed in heaven. The poem became jargon. The poem was the imperfect product of a hasty muse. The poem wanted someone to worship. The poem had a forever feeling. The poem had a feeling that nevermore was here to stay—that, day after day, there would always be more nevermore to contend with. The force of the poem's character was cumulative. The poem carried some kind of chemical load. The poem liked a starched collar. The poem was pretty, stylish, and smart. The poem was tall, dark, and handsome. The poem's aftershave was an assault on the senses. The poem had courage abundantly, which he shared with everyone. The poem was branded a slut before she'd ever been kissed. The poem was bullied into a stutter and a lifelong sleep disorder. Through dark works, the poem became a malcified force. The poem tipped the scales at an even 300 lbs. The poem made a church. The poem spun a basketball on the tip of her finger. An ellipsis brought the poem quickly to a new thought. The poem trusted the sanity of his vessel. The poem was like a didactic bass-line in a classic rock radio tune. There were notable gaps in the poem's CV. The world saw her as an exquisite poem, but the poem's husband saw her as an expert nag. The poem collected dick pics and beaver shots of the famous. The poem was wet with tears, continuous tears from every new reader. The poem was comfortable on stilts. The poem couldn't sit still. The poem was a fourth-grade student's valentine card to a beloved teacher. The poem was positioned primarily as an expression of religious beliefs, but it was a political statement, not prayer. The poem said, God gives and some people take with both hands, leaving little left for the meek and mild. The poem was a found object, naive and sentimental, profound. The poem was a cadaver-sniffing dog. The poem was a standup comedian who wore a baseball cap backwards and told corny jokes—in other words, a natural born

Capricorn. The poem had endometriosis. The poem lived in symbiosis with invasive houseplants. The poem choked on onomatopoeia. The poem referred to his three nieces and two nephews as Satan's litter. The poem was made immortal as an animated character. Like Goldilocks, the poem insisted that her porridge must be just right, not too hot and not too cool. The poem captured glee, imprisoning its base elements. The poem went about in pity for itself, and all the while a great wind carried it across the sky. The poem fetched fresh flowers. The poem was intersex. The poem was a guitar solo before the chorus. The poem objected to the impossibility of sainthood. The poem was a gypsy from a strange and distant time. The poem had wolf blood in its veins. The poem had altogether too much energy. The poem was, in practice, Christian. The poem embraced Buddhism. The poem was a weed whose virtues had not yet been discovered. The poem was an agreeable weed indeed. The poem was written by a racist. When it came to cologne, the poem was a douser. For the poem, too much cologne was never enough. The poem ejaculated prematurely but his refractory period was brief. The poem's new mustache wasn't fooling anyone. The poem never matured. The poem initiated the final countdown. Revenant or zombie, the poem was alive again. The poem was friendly with the idea of socialism. The poem was merely a thought, not an idea. The poem was at ease in a demotic idiom. The poem kept alive in him the glorious spirit of bounding youth. The poem swiped left.

The poem swiped right. The poem definitely had a type. The poem made a stone of her heart. The poem said, Hindsight is 50/50. The poem was an imaginary garden with real toads in it. The poem was the unruly enjambment in the conga line. The poem was terminally pretty. The poem adopted a new putting stance and sank a twelve-foot birdy from the fringe. The poem was brutally handsome. The poem had a nasty reputation as a cruel dude. The poem was at the top, middle, and bottom of the food pyramid. The poem was three servings of fruit and vegetables, a sensible amount of dairy, not too much bread, and just enough protein. The poem was a naked bowl of berries. The poem was a peeled banana, a skinned tangerine, and a scooped melon. The poem was a fruit salad—a word-salad, a jabberwocky. The poem was a diet soft drink. The poem was a liquid diet. The poem was keto. The poem was paleo. The poem was Atkins and then Pritikin. The poem binged, then purged. The poem was a carved pumpkin, a jack-o'-lantern. The poem was a single-minded guy. The poem relied on predicates. The poem was in a subjunctive mood. The poem was criticized for being adverbial. The poem suffered from prolixity. The poem was fact-checked and then published as news that stayed news. The poem was objectively subjective. The poem had a surfeit of testosterone, the result of too much pasta marinara. The poem was like a metaphor. The poem was a simile. The poem revealed God's favorite hiding places. The poem was born and raised in a standard, run-of-the-mill milltown. The poem didn't realize he was weird looking until he saw himself on TV. The poem was an elephant talking. The poem was embarrassed by a show of public affection from his little dog. When the poem rolled her eyes, people died. The poem was dead words on cold paper. The poem thought he had to fuck everyone who wanted to fuck him. The poem thought it had to commemorate every sexual encounter with a poem. Early on, the poem wrote content designed to attract, educate, and convert visitors to customers for a web services company. The poem was well-fed but not fat. The poem savored the taste of his broken heart. The poem humiliated a man who deserved it. The poem was a tight hug, a long embrace. The poem was a précis on reluctancy. The poem had some fancy-schmancy friends with old, old money. The poem was literal. The poem was figurative. The poem was the least-lovable plush toy on a little girl's bed. Across four quatrains, the poem balanced the declarative, the imperative, the exclamatory, and the interrogative. The poem was given to lazy speech patterns. The poem was a sub-prime mortgage. The poem loved a screeching-brakes caesura sound effect. In its first draft, the poem had dashes where important words would be placed later on. The poem was beseeching. The poem was besmirching. The poem was bedazzled on the back of a Nike hoodie. The poem had shit for brains. The poem was a shit magnet. The poem was a report from the afterlife. The poem was needlepointed on a tiny throw-pillow. Oyez, oyez, oyez, the poem began. The poem was a young man, twenty-three years old but without maturity, who played the eccentric to hide gaping flaws in his moral makeup. The poem exemplified the bee, programmed to pollenate. The poem's wax visage was melting. The poem was on a first-name-basis with lonely. The poem was a terms-and-conditions nightmare for readers, securing a perpetual, worldwide, non-exclusive, royalty-free, sublicensable, and transferable license to redistribute, publish, access, use, store, transmit, review, disclose, preserve, extract, modify, reproduce, share, use, display, copy, distribute, translate, transcribe, create derivative works, and process its readers' thoughts and utterances. The poem was dating again, but nothing serious. The poem made a good confession, said an Act of Contrition, two Our Fathers, and a Hail Mary, then, with a clear conscience, received Holy Communion. The poem resembled a constitution, a bill of rights. The poem wandered in grief. The poem had a childlike take on mortality. The poem embraced matrimonial somethingness. The poem mistook horny for happy. The poem corrected cliché misused. The poem was rap, if it was anything. The poem was late and soon. The poem was getting and spending. The poem wallowed in the deep end, preparing to drown. Growing up, the poem couldn't do anything right. The poem grew wings. The poem listed its morning resentments. The poem had thick, hairy arms. The poem had long, shapely legs. The poem had a heart of glass. The poem had two turntables and a microphone. The poem had hands like hatchets. Dandruff salted the poem's shoulders. The poem was all for personification. In fact, personification was the poem's sole reason to live. Without personification—the literal possibility of becoming a person—the poem had no more life in it than an aborted fetus. The poem absorbed all of the lore it saw. The poem had an infallible memory of myth— Greek, Roman, Norse, Celtic, Hindu, Canaanite, Berber, Egyptian, Hittite, Hurrian, Sumerian, Persian, Springsteenian, Marvelian, Bai, Gnostic, Scythian, Mongolian, Tibetan, Samoan, Paleo-Balkan, Estonian, Finnic, Haida, Hopi, Incan, Mayan, Navaho, Wiccan, Zapotec, to name but a few. The poem's own mythology was rational, functional, structural, and psychological. The poem always had good luck. The poem was a gentle laxative. The poem was a riddle in nine syllables. The poem was a joke with a devastating punchline. The poem was a sandwich wrapped in wax paper. The poem repeated its title in the last line, a favorite trick. Daybreak was the title of the poem. There was cat hair on the poem's lap, which meant that she was loved. The poem wanted to be a psychic imperative. The poem clearly expressed mixed feelings. The poem tried living in the real world instead of a shell, but she was bored before she even began. The poem's days were as long as an anchorite's beard. The poem was clear as a windowpane bumped by a bumblebee's head. The poem awoke tired to the bone. The poem was a canny, emendatious editor. All the poem wanted was everything. The poem was an astronaught. The poem's dearest friend said, Bitch don't blink. The poem missed the prison of home. The poem missed the prison of school. The poem's penis was best described as cherubic. Logic played no part in the poem's genesis. The poem was a traveler by trade. The poem had a buoyancy. The poem had wit. The poem was a throat punch. The poem had no siblings and only one cousin. The poem still had a gusto. The poem wore a new pair of gravity boots. The poem examined its emotions. In a loud bar, the poem was always the loudest. The poem was generated by a poem-a-day bot that would be one-hundred years old in the year 2112. The poem was a vampire. The poem was a werewolf. The poem was a zombie. The poem was one of Frankenstein's monsters. The poem was a ghost in a fitted sheet. The poem said, Fuck tha Grammar Police. The poem gambled with the house's money. The poem floated like a butterfly and stung like a bee. The poem summarized its virtues. The poem was between trains. Someone—or some *thing*— undid the poem's sparkle. The poem was a feminine engine. The poem was written with disappearing ink. The poem's blade had grown dull. The poem ignored the stop sign. The poem was exposed to a new colloquialism. The poem's heart was colder than a well-digger's ass. There was panic in the poem's voice. The only wish that ever came true for the poem was his cremation. The poem was a reverse mortgage. The poem was a flawless meal, everything cooked to perfection, served elegantly, and consumed with loved ones. The poem was an effective digestive. The poem's feet were semipalmated.

The poem had style like the *Chicago Manual of Style*. A judge threatened the poem with contempt of court. The poem was comfortable in the knowledge that everyone felt more or less the same most of the time. The poem dated more once she lowered her standards. The poem was in a waiting room in her gynecologist's office, and she told herself that she was a lady-in-waiting. The poem identified as subject and predicate. The poem was queer that way. The poem was a cis gender male. The poem was all woman, too much woman for most men. The poem was va-va-va-voooom. The poem had some baggage. The poem unpacked a disordered overnight bag. The poem watched a *Quantum of Solace*, hoping for just a little bit of entertainment. The poem had feet of clay. The poem dicked around with a pantoum. The poem was a stress eater. At hiding, the poem was expert. The poem went a-courtin' and he did ride, uh-hunh. The poem had a sword and pistol by his side. The poem was breast-fed until he was six years old. The poem was a milkman. The poem was retired now. The poem measured the fullness of time. The poem was flat-footed. The poem deleted a work in progress accidentally. The poem won a backgammon tournament on a technicality. The poem got a chemistry set for Christmas in his sophomore year in high school. The poem's behavior was frowned upon. The poem felt herself judged. The poem put down roots in a new town. The poem posted a letter to his editor. The poem sent an email to the department chair. The poem texted with his grown children. The poem took the masculine form in most grammars. Some nights, the poem cried and cried and cried. The lock on the poem's diary was decorative. In high school, the poem was intentionally a non-entity. The poem was certain that she would one day do something superhuman. The poem was a living thing. The poem was resuscitated twice at a New Year's Eve party. The poem was once bitten, twice shy. The poem tied up loose ends. The poem told the truth, but told it slant. The poem was caffeine-free. The poem wore a nicotine patch to kick the habit. The poem played the part of an unwelcomed guest. The poem traded a walk on part in a war for a lead role in a cage. The poem diagnosed her mental illness. The poem was a neat freak. The poem was a world trapped inside a person. The poem trapped itself. The poem was asked to leave a gentlemen's club. The poem ordered a club sandwich at her father's club. The poem waited in line to get into the popular dance club, his hand resting on a velvet rope. The poem protested the clubbing of baby seals. The poem tried on a crown at a costume store. The only real crown ever worn by the poem was a cuckold's horns. In researching cuckoldry, the poem learned that bunny ears made by holding two fingers behind an unwitting man's head were meant to reveal the secret that his wife had been unfaithful. The poem felt the lightning and waited on the thunder. The poem was a prison escape movie. The poem was a goth teen. The poem was a gossip girl. The poem was a pixie. The poem was a sprite. The poem was a changeling. The poem was a lollygagger. The poem sang "Tiptoe Through the Tulips." The poem was having a wonderful time. The poem smashed a ukulele onstage. The poem was pure energy. The poem was powered by a solar sex panel. The poem didn't moralize. The poem stepped into the changing room to change. The poem was a sweet old gal with a wide fanny. The poem recalled singing "Danny Boy" after a long night of drinking. The poem's arms were around the future, and his back was against the past. Music transported the poem into song. The poem shook himself out of a perseverating dream. The poem typed as fast as possible and gave no regard to punctuation or proper spelling until the point of exhaustion was achieved. The poem never refused cocaine. The poem distrusted all instruments of measure. The poem had a laissez faire attitude on the creation, dissemination, and consumption of literature. The poem's mother often called him an idiotic creature. The poem was an irregular verb. The poem was an improper fraction. The poem was an indifferent teacher. The poem was an impertinent question. The poem was an idea that was not embraced. The poem was an adverb of degrees. The poem was an adjective of scale. The poem was an instantiation on, of all things, love. The poem translated feet into meter. The poem converted strange currencies into U.S. dollars. The poem petered out. The poem sallied forth. The poem was johnny-on-the-spot. The poem, like a lazy Susan, was misnomered. The poem talked on many too many topics for many too many hours. The poem was seething with laughter. The poem adhered to the golden mean and practiced the golden nice. The poem overheard its name spoken in praise. The poem was derided in the *Times*. The poem was not on social media. The poem was on statins. The poem was often invited but rarely welcomed. The poem's dawn devotional was delayed by the late-rising sun. There was one lie that the poem loved so much he married it. The poem indulged in its lore, played it up as both an essential feature and an adjunct benefit. The poem understood the last nostalgia. The poem remembered when rock was young. The poem was made of common clay. The poem personified everything. The poem worked so hard he had a heart attack. There was nothing especially special about the poem. The poem had quite a tongue—it was canine in length. The thing that disturbed the poem was the low spark of high-heeled boys. When the poem's search for logic failed, she knew, finally, and with certainty, that she was a poem. The poem knew that the 80/20 rule applied across all matters of business, personal finance, romance, education, sports betting, seasonal weather. The poem was known to have thin skin. The poem ordered fries with her shake. The poem was a thing of beauty, a joy forever. The poem felt sometimes like a restaurant that had lots of tables but no chairs. The poem woke early to feed her fish and water her plants. In photographs, the poem always looked helpless. The poem was a raised ranch, a split-level. The poem flourished in a terrarium's small environment water cycle. The poem pushed a boulder up an inclined plane. The poem used a lever to move a cold heart in a new direction. The poem was a system of pulleys that obviated the weight of each line. The poem predated the wheel and the axle as well. The poem screwed his landlady. The poem utilized all six simple machines in revising a villanelle. The poem was a scratch ticket. The poem was encircled by a Venn diagram that included 100% of the areas of two unknown data sets. The poem was complex as a seed. The poem was the lone full-time staff member at a busy complaint department in a mid-size department store in receivership. Exhaustion trumps infinity, said the poem. The poem was as wallpaper, decorative, an interior design alternative to paint. In a roomful of big tits, the poem's tits were always the biggest. The poem had a messy life, which she delighted in. The poem didn't have an inside voice. The poem never left the playground. The poem was a dapper fellow. The poem was a colicky baby. The poem stopped at the horse and buggy, imagining no further transportation innovation. The poem was told to stop but would not stop. The poem grew in two directions—up where it could be seen and down to the depths—below root-level—where it could not be seen. The poem was sicker than his secrets. The poem was in recovery. The poem was a slave to love. The poem was a slave to fashion. The poem was a slave to the beat. The poem would have masturbated to death, but there are only twenty-four hours in a day. Death gave the poem authority. The poem said, Pardon me all over the place. The poem wasn't what it looked like. Facially, the poem resembled a beaver. The poem orbited earth, and vice-versa. The poem would orbit anything orbitable. The poem was a planet. The poem was a star. Big words made the poem's heart beat faster. The poem was one word too many to be a drabble. The poem reached the age of consent in a few regressive states. The poem was late with her period. The poem was refuted by data scientists at MIT. The poem counted only five toppings on her everything bagel—sesame seeds, poppy seeds, dried garlic, dried onions, and kosher salt. The poem wanted to redefine the word everything. The poem lost herself trying to be everything to everyone. The poem turned everything into a poem. The poem turned to the thesaurus to find a synonym for everything. The poem said, Anything is encompassed by everything. The poem didn't know how to stop herself from turning everything into a poem. The poem had hope on its side, and that was everything. The poem had a mission, and that was everything. When the poem finally fell in love, it was everything she had dreamt it would be. The poem's weakness was every living thing. The poem was a small, slim woman with insect legs in black yoga pants. The poem's flipflops percussively exaggerated her quick stride. The poem's hair looked like she'd just left a good salon. The poem wished and hoped and planned and plotted and waited. The poem defied gravity. The poem didn't know much about purses, but he thought that his wife's new purse looked expensive. The poem's wife loved him on payday. The poem was one of a million poems, but the poem was still special. The poem was a sing-along, and everybody knew the words. The poem had a kissing rhyme. The poem felt like an unsatisfied, deflated sex doll. The poem ordered the seven coordinating conjunctions from best to worst: and, for, so, or, nor, but, yet. The poem hated yet because it helped the second clause of the sentence forsake the first. The poem was a talkative taxi driver. The poem put all its faith into a sestina. The poem was consumed with delight. If the poem was not an introvert or an extrovert, then the poem was a pervert. The poem wanted to take back the last decade. The poem made actions into nouns. The poem was featured in the local newspaper more than a few times. The poem wanted to travel to the planet where all the dogs came from. The poem was sweet as pie but her title was profane. The poem was a heroic couplet. As a schoolchild, the poem engaged in parallel play with her classmates, not really joining in their games. The poem would do anything to avoid boredom. The poem was a face-eating bear. The poem proffered sexual good tidings to all. The poem worked as a soda jerk in a retro-themed diner. The poem had false teeth. The poem put on false eyelashes—it was Saturday night! The poem had artificial breasts. The poem shaved her pussy. The poem ate a lot of pussy and sucked a lot of cock in her day. The poem was a tasty strumpet. The poem looked hot in a short skirt. The poem made depression cute. The poem's vocabulary grew. The poem was an epic of no consequence. From a bench beside the river, the poem watched the joggers jog and the fisherman fish. The poem was a clown who personified jollity and symbolically represented the triumph of mirth over misery. The poem was an unhappy clown married to an unfaithful woman, but he resolved to schtick it out for the sake of their children. The poem was a natural born contortionist, flexible as an elastic band. The poem was suspicious of charity. The poem's first beard grew in white. The poem's autonym reflected their gender identification and the power of their self-possession. The poem cost one penny, but it was not for sale. The poem began a journey of one thousand poems with one poem. The poem was radically conventional. The poem was intergalactic, planetary. The poem identified as queer. The poem wanted to leave her body to science, but only to a mad scientist. The poem was composed in a cemetery and later revised in a coffeehouse. The poem was a waterlogged soccer ball. The poem was programmed with a self-destruct algorithm. The poem had no soul to call its own. The poem sank to the bottom of the ocean. The poem was through with love. The poem didn't need pleasure anymore. The poem revealed the terror inside clocks. The poem was a surprisingly agile lover. The poem quickly became acclimated to its new surroundings. The poem was courting a venture capitalist. The poem's personal economy was slightly more than zero dollars. The poem was a stress eater. The poem was a bit of a clothes horse. The poem had a great memory for rock concerts—set lists, opening acts, friends who came along. The poem had two babies in her belly. The poem lived in regret. The poem was inside specially marked boxes of a popular breakfast cereal. The poem hyperlinked to a website offering discount vacation getaways. The poem hyperventilated for the sake of hyperventilation. The poem was becoming less human, more divine. The poem was today years old when he learned that you can't shit a shitter. The poem was a cuckold. The poem was a bear. When the poem's eyes faced front, she was ready to hunt. When the poem's eyes looked to each side, she knew it was time to run and hide. The poem's destiny was to be the king of pain. The poem was a constitutional monarchy. The poem leaned socialist. The poem hid in the tall grass. The poem slipped his fingers into a pair of brass knuckles. In considering AI, the poem felt kinship with John Henry and his hammer. The poem had tuberculosis but nursed itself back to health. In the fullness of time, the poem was nearly half-full. The poem was running on empty. Once lit, the poem was like one of those trick birthday candles that can't be blown out. The poem was unstuck in time, traveling forward and backward. The poem paid attention to everything, everyone. The poem had a solution for all the golems that were proliferating in his corner of the planet. The poem said, You *can* judge a *banned* book by its cover. The poem smoked wherever she wanted to. The poem smoked like a chimney. The poem played drinking games with glee and abandon. The poem admitted defeat—it wasn't so bad. The poem always remembered and would never forget that the Uniform Code to create an obelisk on a PC is ALT + 0134, and OPT +3 on a Mac. Something inside the poem was burning. The poem was gorgeous by any measure. The poem was higher than a kite. The poem was the extant journal of a sea creature living on land and yearning to fly. The poem was a shy little thing with a wild side. The poem was a late bloomer. The poem got the giggles. The poem had the hiccups. The poem had the angina. The poem fought in the chocolate wars. The poem was interested in laziness as expressed by the wealthy. The poem was one of those guys who got pee-shy at public urinals. The poem was a child actor in Hollywood and, really, she never grew up. The poem aimed an arrow at the evil heart of conformity. The poem's right arm was in a sling again. The poem was the sole proprietor of a beachside sandwich shoppe. The poem's DNA was all over the bedsheets and the pillowcase. The poem was rain on the roof. The poem finally owned a home with central air conditioning. The poem was a flat-rate auto mechanic. The poem jumped in the river forever. The poem was stately, plump. The poem was palpable and mute as a globed fruit. The poem was a Christmas tree on Christmas Day in the morning. The poem was figgy pudding. The poem was getting jiggy with it. The poem was a long-haul trucker leading an interstate convoy. The poem didn't take drugs; the poem *was* drugs. The poem's tautology was inelegant but effective. The poem's research on shadows was sketchy. The poem was palely loitering outside the walls of the city. The poem was a cat with a long tail who liked to make a show of its tail but gave off an aggressive don't-touch-my-tail vibe. The poem was about a cat, written by a cat. The poem didn't dare use a possessive pronoun when she talked about the cat that lived with her. The poem was a hairless cat. The poem was a copycat. A cat had got the poem's tongue. A cat scan showed the poem's brain fog. The poem was an indoor cat. The poem read a description of her work that she found instructive. The poem was an oil painting of Henry James. The poem was a juggler. The poem was missing a few teeth. The poem was a failed picnic. The poem never learned to swim. The poem devised a death-row menu for his last meal—fried clams, French fries, lemonade, vanilla ice cream. The poem was a nuptial, concluding that marriage is errands. The poem's password was wordpass. The poem had a naturally sexy way of walking—it was something in her hips, completely unaffected. The poem had an even sexier walk that she used when she wanted to attract attention on the streets. Obviously, the poem was about poetry. The poem was labelled word-salad by a dieting critic. The poem was everything on the menu. The poem fell in love every five minutes. The poem's menstruations were mild most months, as long as she ate right, got sleep, and hydrated sufficiently. The poem lit one cigarette after the other. The poem trained the voice in his head to call himself Buddy—like, Hey, Buddy, why don't you get yourself a nice cup of tea and sit down for a spell. The poem was a self-workshopping poem. The poem was a connecting flight. The poem was outta sight! The poem's problem with the dead was that the dead don't stay dead. Death gave the poem a new and everlasting authority. The poem farmed a hot half-acre in hell. The poem was a youth no more. The poem rocked the bells. The poem could play the guitar just like a-ringin' a bell. The poem was a civics lesson. The poem was a government of laws, not of men. The poem applied some blue chalk to the tip of its pool cue, sized up the eight ball. The poem was a summer surprise. The poem was concerned with winter. The poem was a trumpet for summer. The poem fell into autumn. The poem had a mind of winter. The poem had a summery heart. The poem had spring in its steps. The poem was prone to fall. The poem was a true believer. The poem was a seer, a sage. The poem was a cranky mofo. The poem had a sweet lisp that made her every recited line sound precious. The poem began with because. The poem had entered the horse latitudes. The poem rode a painted pony. Wop bop a loo bop a lop bam boom was the poem's opening salvo. The poem was a strangler. The poem took a bow. The poem relished a rare victory lap. The poem was in disguise as flash fiction. The poem had a Roman nose. The poem was a *bildungsroman.* The poem was a roman à clef. The poem was a *räuberroman.* The poem was a Roman Holiday. The poem was a Roman Catholic, lapsed. At times the poem was a

74

rondeau and, at times, a rondel. The poem was raunchy in speech, had a locker-room sensibility. The poem applauded the legalization of cannabis in her home state. The poem was a sour burp. The poem slurped her soup. The poem poked at her steak. The poem went hither and yon, topic-wise. The poem had a sun protective factor equal to that of corduroy. The poem worshipped a hammer. The poem liked to go about topless. The poem's lines were not elegant, but they were true. The poem made an assertion that he was not worthy of what he desired. The poem, like the sun, was daily new and old. The poem sounded an alarum. The poem wasted energy examining and expressing her feelings, not acting on them. The poem was a tax loophole. The poem suppressed an instinct for prayer. The poem was a monument to humility. The poem played the glockenspiel like an angel possessed by the divine. The poem was ambidextrous. The poem was a nation of one. The poem rested her head on a surrealistic pillow and dreamed of the sounds of color and the light of a sigh. Face first, the poem was jowling into middle age. The poem had entered reverse puberty—she refused to call it menopause. The poem's innate kindliness would not become activated until he reached old age. When she was a teen, the poem rode horses bareback, no saddle and no reins. The poem refused to perform cunnilingus, because he believed it was women's work. The poem was a quiet woman with loud tattoos. The poem was a virtual reproduction of her mother, no matter how hard she resisted. The poem was the top daily news headline every day for years and years. The poem had a winning smile. The poem was a secular saint. The poem said, I want to say more, but not now. The poem was autotelic. The poem contained a mantra, free of charge, not that anyone noticed. The poem woke with a gorgeous lump under the blankets of his bed, and he could not remember her name. The poem was a gunslinger. The poem was a gluegunslinger. The poem was the second-to-last ronin. The poem objected to the marginalization of adverbs. The poem's hard drive was nearly full. The poem spied with his little eye a pair of dice rolled to Snake Eyes—a terrible two. The poem gave name to every dice combination—Craps for three, Little Joe for four, five was Fever, six was Big Six, seven was called Natural, eight was good ole Ada from Decatur, nine was Nina, ten was known as Big Dick, eleven was also called Natural, and twelve was known as Boxcars. There was a proliferation of fabrications in the poem's vast notes on the subject of truth in composition. The poem said, Feel sad but don't *be* sad. The poem was accused of being a puppet, so the poem simply said, Not a puppet. The poem resisted editing. The poem was enamored of its prolixity. The poem was cut on the bias, elasticizing the warp and weft of its fabric. The poem invented whataboutism. The poem had manga eyes. The poem was a kind billionaire, the rarest type of billionaire. The poem was a funicular that carried passengers high above a slew of roadside attractions. The poem was a minestrone, theme-wise. The poem was a minefield of self-doubt. Symbolism would be the death of the poem. The poem shared its joys and burdens. The poem announced its pansexuality, and enjoyed the attendant head-scratching. When the poem was a teenager, he longed for one of his dates to give him a handjob because he had yet to learn there was such a thing as a blowjob. The poem had been from Tucson to Tucumcari, and from Tehachapi to Tonopah. The poem had driven every kind of rig that had ever been made. The poem had driven the backroads so it wouldn't get weighed. The poem asked to be given weed, whites, and wine. The poem asked to be shown a good time. The poem was willin' even when weary. The poem was not amused. The poem was ambushed on a night just like this. The poem showed no haste. The poem took its time. The poem only made a move when it was good and ready. The poem gave readers mild vertigo. The poem gave readers serenity. The poem posited a theory regarding the afterlife that was wholly devoted to gratification of the soul. The poem was a holiday in the sun. The poem kissed reason goodbye. The poem flicked some imaginary dust off her shoulder. The poem didn't want anything to change between him and his son. The poem was a gifted monologist. The poem put a pencil to his temple. The poem wished to be reincarnated as a pictogram. The poem had an hourglass figure, all hips and nips. The poem had an unforgiving nature. The poem knew more than it was letting on. The poem preferred to think of himself as an orphan. The poem was superior in translation. The poem had joy. The poem had fun. The poem had seasons in the sun. The poem was removed from the reading comprehension section of the Scholastic Aptitude Test. The poem's car had a manual transmission. The poem's prions were attacking her from inside the building that was her body. The poem's pronouns were *blech* and *meh* and *mine*. The poem's middle name was Gimme. Yes, the poem was selfish (more often than not). The poem's father had a hunting dog that could not be treated as a pet, was considered a weapon. The poem took ecstasy at a rave. The poem smoked dope at her one and only Grateful Dead concert. The poem took a sleeping aid when traveling. The poem had a Homeric daily commute. The poem had a thing for natural redheads, but only the pretty ones. The court ruled that the poem was mad. The poem invited everyone on the bus to sing along. The poem supported not just one hanger-on but many. The poem followed a star but still got lost. The poem had no use for the pickaxe that was in the shed of the first home she bought on her own. The poem was an anthem to the American muscle cars of the late sixties. If it doesn't come naturally, leave it, said the poem. Some readers had an adverse reaction to the poem. At most, the poem was a peripheral figure in the indie lit scene. When the poem had not achieved meaning, the poem would add a verse and another verse. The poem confused apogee with perigee, sturm with drang. The poem hated vacations. If an airline can reschedule a hundred flights in one afternoon, then the poem could reschedule his semi-annual check-up with his dentist. The poem reneged on a scheduled reading appearance at a school a hundred miles away. A fellow poem was being a bit too palsy-walsy with the poem. In truth, the poem had no subtext. The poem was opaque. Nobody understood how simple the poem was. For some, the poem was a lucky charm. The magnifying mirror brought tears to the poem's eyes. The poem would not delineate frown lines from smile lines. The poem was left out of the Norton Anthology. The poem had a cruel streak. The poem had a pair of cruel shoes from the 1970s. The poem wanted to be sedated. The poem had a fearful symmetry. The poem applied lip liner to her beauty mark to make it more symmetrical and to center it on her cheek. The poem thought of a number between one and two. The poem had a dream about mushrooms, and it was trippy. The poem let the day begin in absentia. Hungover, the poem stepped into the shower with her bra still on. The poem was not gay so much as it was not particularly straight. The poem had a paint chip on its shoulder. The poem reviewed the syllabus and shrank at the sight of student oral presentations scheduled during the last week of the semester. The poem would not simulate ardor. The lines of the poem could be read in any order and still make perfect sense. The poem had an airtight alibi. The poem meant to say bunt cake, but she reversed the first letters and, well, she shocked her beloved aunt by saying cunt bake. Spoonerisms would be the death of the poem. The poem's knees jellied when a handsome boy in her workshop said, in a tentative whisper, Enjambment. The poem was not actually about a woodpile. The poem was just like a pile of leaves. The poem voted yes on the controversial steakhouse initiative. The poem sipped white wine from a fine green goblet. To emphasize the accuracy of his witty rejoinder, the poem mimed the throwing of a dart—bullseye! The poem redeemed $1.20 deposit on a case of empty beer cans, and applied that to the purchase of a case of cold beer. The poem was the reason and the remedy. After years of neglect, the poem was being read again. The poem wore a matador's suit of lights. The poem caucused with voters from her district. The poem was quite impervious to threats. The poem had a great fall. The poem plucked the wings from painted butterflies, to fan moonbeams from his sleepy eyes. The poem danced and danced and danced. The poem swayed through the crowd to an empty space. The poem was a young, sweet prince. The poem liked strong coffee and weak tea. Growing up, the poem was a latch-key kid, and that feeling never left her. The poem's dearest friend was a little boy called Jackie Paper. The poem's dearest wish was to once again have a child's mind. The poem was a hopeful futilitarian. The poem was an agent of futility. The poem bathed in pathos. For decades, the poem dined on an emerging writer's award. The poem was written against fondant. The poem baked another cake. The poem ate a fried baloney sandwich. The poem was a mysterious kind of folk. The poem was curious, not judgmental. The poem had an absolute emotional honesty. The ghost of Hamlet's father called out to the poem, Oy! The poem was a ransom note of complicated directions. The poem ached to deploy the word forsooth. The poem concluded that the juice was not worth the squeeze. As a *Jeopardy!* contestant, the poem refused to frame his answers in the form of a question. The poem's legs were cellulite free. The poem owned a beaded vest that never left its hanger in the back of her deep closet. Florists never charged the poem for flowers. The poem had a vocabulary for beauty. The poem was a quadratic equation, its variables rearrangeable. The poem wanted it both ways, like most women. The poem was a bad mamma jamma. There was a famine of ideas and the poem was obese. The poem's new lover dressed only in black, which is a red flag according to a popular dating advice website. The poem was a noble hermit. The poem wasn't fighting anymore. The poem was surrendering. The poem whispered sweet nothings into a thousand ears. The poem didn't need a shrink. The poem needed an exorcist. When she needed to defend her body, the poem would say, My tits might be fake, but my ass is real. The poem was a malady. The poem was a cyst. The poem had a string of health scares. The poem had a headache. Nobody was paying any attention to the poem. What did the poem have to do to be seen, actually *seen*. The poem collected trinkets from her travels. The poem benefited from the deaths of loved ones and strangers alike. The poem picked its nose. The poem was a pauper with holes in his pockets. The poem was a beggar, always with his hand out. Every photo of the poem looked like a mugshot. Legally, the poem was toast. The poem was dedicated to a sullen woman. The poem lived in a doll's house—it was that small. The poem asked God for a sign. The poem asked Siri who won Major League Baseball's Triple Crown in 1967. The poem asked love to be true. The poem swore an oath. The poem recited The Pledge of Allegiance. The poem was composed entirely of interrogatives. The poem was questioning. The poem was questionstruck. The poem was in recovery. The poem angrily explained the difference between a choice and a decision—these two words were almost antonyms. The poem named a child, and that child changed its name. The poem named a cat, and that cat ran away. The poem named a new feeling, and that feeling was fleeting. The poem amplified an overlooked sentiment. The poem deployed subterfuge in protection of the child that still lived inside his heart. The poem coupled with a couplet. The poem was a streetwalker, that is, a lady of the night, a hooker, a prostitute, a venereal. Even the poem's farts rhymed. The poem was a gassy old coot. The trick to the poem's unique speed-reading technique was to absorb topic sentences only and ignore everything else on the page. The poem spoke to the incarcerated. There was not a day when the poem did not look upon something new in the world. The poem lived in the library. The poem fought in a war. The poem was a deserter. The poem was less than macho. The poem married two fools in one lifetime. The poem gave energy to some readers but depleted others. The poem skipped rope to lose weight. The poem hopscotched from one subject to another, surefooted, nimble. The poem diagrammed sentences to fight insomnia. The poem resembled a bar graph fallen on its side. The poem was the reincarnation of a poison pen. The poem had been drinking all morning, and was now ready to write. The poem did battle with demons, real and imaginary. The poem did little more than sigh from time to time. The poem came to life through a tender gesture. The poem took flight with a feather in her hair. The poem was on a PSYOP assignment for the FBI, collecting information and disseminating disinformation. The poem loved a parade. Hallelujah was the word wet on the poem's lips. The poem's arrow missed the bull's-eye by a cunt hair. The poem came by his blackeye honestly. The poem was survived only by its secrets. The poem sang about the rhetoric of failure. It was a whole hullabaloo, the poem noted. There was a measure of spite in every line of the poem. The poem had a tickle in its throat that was resolved with a cough. The poem was written by the poet laureate of Never-Neverland. The poem threw his weight around. The poem's constipation was epic. The poem had a hairy back and a thick neck. The poem was a bill of particulars. It is what it is, said the poem. The poem was neither a fox nor a hedgehog. The poem was tired and wanted to go to bed. The poem went cold turkey and shouldn't have. The poem was climbing the walls. The poem felt a fire in its head. The poem was sick unto death of his own thoughts. The poem sold memories to the forgetful. The poem pressed record on her Dictaphone. The poem hit the snooze button on her alarm. The poem produced a few fresh lines each day. The poem was running low on rhymes. The poem's salivary glands dried up, were totally bankrupt of spit. The poem cursed a new speed bump in the mall parking lot. Like Jesus, the poem was betrayed by one of his apostles. Like Jesus, the poem turned the other cheek for more of the same. Like Jesus, the poem wept at the appointed hour. Like Jesus, the poem was crucified and rose from the dead. Like Jesus, the poem liked to remind those who would listen that he was crucified for *their* sins. Like Jesus, the poem liked to remind attractive women that he looked good on the cross. Except for the long hair and beard, the poem was nothing like Jesus. The poem was a cutter. The poem's story was over, and its rhyme was done. The poem was a people-pleaser but also a misanthrope. The poem lived in dilemma. The poem recalled every house on his paper route. The poem had a feeling, and that's what it was all about. The poem qualified for a tournament of champions. The poem cast aspersions without discrimination. Believe it or not, the poem carried an aroma, and it was a heavy lift. Under the setting sun, the poem touched a hundred flowers but did not pick one. The poem came to understand forever in what would be the final February of his long life. The poem was a sizable portion of beef on a generous plate of greens. The poem liquified under heat and agitation. The poem met a billionaire at a university fundraiser and they had an awkward conversation about legalizing most forms of sex work. The poem was a protracted puberty. The poem liked to please himself more than he wanted to please others. The poem was selfish at times. No matter how hard the poem tried to express the knowledge of his heart and give to the world the gift of song, he knew all of his efforts were a striving after the wind. The poem's desires were fed by loneliness. Pound for pound, the poem was the best prizefighter on the planet. The poem relied on the kindness of strangers. The poem remained a holy virgin all of her days. The poem bought a pair of cheap sunglasses at the drugstore. The poem bought drugs in the park. The poem was about God and rage. The poem was appropriated from an ancient liturgy. The poem's product was depression. The poem's byproduct was fatigue. The poem was done with discipline. The poem was stolen from a busy parking lot, driven to a chop-shop, then sold for parts. At last, the poem was in repose. The poem filled mouths with the taste of a sour grape, a sour apple, and a whiskey sour. The poem inserted another quarter, but it appeared the jinx machine was out of order. The poem was a big yellow taxi. The poem always selected Uber Black. The poem held its breath when crossing bridges. The poem crossed the River Styx. The poem pitched pennies against a dirty sidewalk. After the poem saw the bright lights of

New York City, she knew she would never go back to the farm. The poem was inert in a book until it was read. The poem lived between thought and expression. The poem took a brief residency in the head of its readers. The poem would be happy if three or four people in the world were no more. The poem was a pastiche of Cards Against Humanity. The poem was made from Monopoly cards. The poem was a collection of board games. The poem was about a fish learning how to swim. The poem's Plan B was alcoholism. Nobody lifted a finger to save the poem from its redundancy. The poem was a loaded question. The poem was a loaded gun. The poem was a loaded diaper. The poem was a loaded washing machine. The poem was a pair of loaded dice. The poem was loaded with stardust. The poem tried to catch herself whenever she was being judgmental, particularly when she was being judgmental of another female poem. The poem was most alive in contradiction. Somewhere, a frothy disco version of the poem was dancing the night away. The poem's objectivity was absolute. The poem was sticky—in the larger sense of that concept. The poem was cancerous, a natural carcinogen. The poem's laugh was infectious, particularly in movie theaters. The poem's laugh echoed that of a prospector who never struck gold but loved the folly of the pickaxing and alluvial panning. The poem viewed its impending senility as a late-life adventure. The poem owned space and time. The poem struck a contrapposto pose, with all of her weight on one foot and her shoulders off-axis with her hips. The poem was all change. The poem's superpower was sleep. The poem watched the moon around the house. The poem distrusted all maths—double-entry bookkeeping was at the top of that list. The poem brought her dog to the dog park. New inspiration eluded the poem. The poem was sad to realize it wasn't love, this new thing. The poem wasn't mean, but life was. Sometimes, the poem didn't know what it meant. The poem defied explication. The poem was a surprisingly good inflight movie. The poem was hardwired for disruption. The poem filled in the blanks on its family's medical history. The poem hopped, skipped, and jumped. The poem leapfrogged over an untold number of frogs and toads alike. The poem didn't care where it shat. The poem talked shit about everyone. Much of what the poem knew was learned on tv. The poem perused his bookshelf and record collection to make a desert island list of books and record albums, at the request of an online literary journal. The poem imagined an image and then made it come to life. The poem teetered between willfulness and reluctancy. You're a little firecracker, an old man told the poem. The poem wanted a bride but did not need a wife. The poem noted that there were many things that could *not* be had as one or another but only together, as a pair. The poem gave the devil his due. The poem prayed more than any other mental activity. The poem bid you pray from matins to vespers, nonstop. A preoccupation with strippers would be the poem's undoing. There had been a stitching and unstitching of the poem, and it had come to naught. The poem didn't expect to be so bright and bon vivant so far from home. No matter how hard he worked to make sweet sounds with words, the poem would always be thought an idler by bankers, schoolmasters, and clergymen. The poem was the bristling reaction that signaled the end of something—the end of everything. The poem had another toothache. The poem would die toothless. The poem would be reincarnated as the Tooth Fairy. The poem would die penniless. The poem died with a needle in her arm. The poem reincarnated in the form of a nap. The poem regenerated its tail. Like a pinned butterfly, the poem was displayed in a suffocating cloche. The poem was a fight song for pacifists. The poem gave up, caved in, surrendered, to a cavity search at the airport. The poem refused to believe that Keats didn't rhyme with Yeats. The poem was always busy being born. The poem was dying of malignancy. The poem had a roommate in college who was born on third base, and he mistakenly thought he'd hit a triple. The poem was an onslaught of adjectives. The poem played devil's advocate for the much-maligned adverb. The poem was every part of speech, every tense, all usages. The poem wore a red fright wig to a midnight screening of *Stephen King's It*. The poem was cucked and cucked again. Full disclosure: The poem was lovelier than a tree. The poem strived to say in the best way possible all that had to be said. The poem courted heartbreak. The poem consistently lost his heart to women who were way out of his league. The poem knew her heart to be a thick clutch of muscle, lopsided, mute. Don't waste your prayers on me because I'm already a fucking saint, the poem wrote in a prison letter to his ailing mother. The poem found footing on the balance beam and learned to walk a straight line. The poem made the sound of a trumpeting elephant on its way to the zoo. The poem climbed a tree and fell out of it accidentally on purpose, for the experience. The poem skipped to the lou. The poem was like a broken vase that had been very well repaired. The poem was one of those poems that people have forever argued about. The poem wasn't as kindly as everyone believed. The poem presaged the advent of hook-up apps. The poem timed how long it took the traffic light to change its mind. The poem said, A stop sign never changes its mind. The poem kissed a lot of fools. The poem fooled a lot of fools. The poem was crucified upside-down à la Saint Peter. The poem's fashion choices were unassailable. The poem had the inseam of a man, 32 inches. The poem shoplifted makeup and tiny bottles of liquor. The poem wanted to be interested in someone. The poem didn't want someone to be interested in her. The poem wore out her first library card. The poem sometimes broke into song at the laundromat. The poem was a taciturn Cancer. The poem could not be unsaid unmade unthought unknown undefined untrued. The poem was dancing with his darling to the "Tennessee Waltz" when automatic gunfire erupted. With a shrug, the poem clarified her position on premarital sex. The poem crawled to the Annual Ugly Bug Ball. The poem flew through customs, despite the eight-ball of cocaine in his toiletries bag. A fish hook fit inside the poem's open eye. The poem wanted more *Gilmore Girls* in her life, less *Gossip Girl.* The poem wore a t-shirt that said: Dress like Lorelei, Think like Rory, Drink like Emily, Cook like Sookie, Rock like Lane, Talk like Paris. The poem could not get his wife and daughters to agree that Emily Gilmore was also a Gilmore Girl. The poem had receipts, first drafts. No one knew why the poem stuck out her tongue at the sight of a camera. The poem was a supply-side text chain. A certain song had worn a groove into the poem's heart. The poem was flush with Greek allusions. The poem flashed a wad of foreign currency. The poem went all in when he should have folded. The crown didn't fit the poem's extra-large head. The poem's stream of consciousness was orderly, adjusting to his mental health. The poem had well more than a pocketful of poesy. The poem drank one for sorrow, two for joy. The poem was more than its collective grammar. The poem was a noun of great renown. The poem was a noun acting as a verb. The poem was a proper noun who often acted as an improper verb. Interviewers ask the poem more questions about his dreadlocks than his words. The poem's heart was so big—so big and strong—he didn't need any of his other organs. The poem repeated itself under stress. People yield to repetition, said the poem. The poem had a health scare that made her work furious.

The poem believed there was a bad moon on the rise. The poem liked the way her jet-lagged mind worked, slowly yet surprisingly assuredly. The poem's hands looked older than her face. The poem faced menopause like a warrior and a worrier. The poem had a fear of an internal avalanche. When the poem did not go to church, he trusted God to understand. The poem reviewed security footage of his alien abduction. The poem's heart was running out of beats. The poem was an inveterate cacographer. The poem was a dog with too big ears. The poem slept through graduate school. The poem wasn't on speaking terms with anyone in her family. The poem was big as a bear and smelled like one, too. On stilts, the poem felt superior yet vulnerable. The poem was an unmade bed. The poem lingered over a second Manhattan, waiting for the bar to close and the bartender to be free. The poem prayed to sin no more and to avoid the near occasion of sin. Those who knew the poem described him as a soft-spoken man, mild-mannered, easy-going. Whatever angst the poem had, it was saved for the page. The page was where the poem came to life. The poem took a pornographic turn. The poem depicted penetration. The poem drew an alternative alphabet. The poem was a grey-green moth, not a gaily-colored butterfly. The poem ate a funsize Snickers bar from his daughter's Halloween haul. The poem required readers to be equally drunk. Tequila had a fortifying effect on the poem. Having been baptized by fire, the poem felt her soul protected against the temporal life. The poem had a tender moment with a bartender who had preternaturally large ears. Take a day off, the poem's boss said. In elementary school, the poem had a friend named Mandy, whose parents had named her after the song by Barry Manilow. Without permission, the poem fell in love and set to writing fragrant lines. The poem was as smug as a 3-D printer. The poem had a talent for coming up with nicknames that stuck. The poem considered his dyslexia an uncredited collaborator. The poem penned another thirteen-ways poem, then edited it down to three things. There was an itch in the palm of the poem's hand, which meant money was coming her way. Taylor Swift broke the poem's heart. The poem knew how to rock a graphic t-shirt. The poem survived for decades after its death, and it was revived after a second death to live again for ages and ages. The poem's wife scratched at her nose—she was spoiling for a fight. The poem's husband acquiesced quickly, which is why she loved him so. The poem killed a prehistoric insect inside his tent. A lover compared the poem to the tide—she comes and goes. The poem documented swamp life. The poem was a sinner in the hands of an angry God. The poem listed the names and an identifying quality of each one of Squanto's brothers: Sprinto was the fastest brother; Slanto had crooked eyes and his left shoulder was two inches higher than his right; Splinto broke his arm repeatedly and always seemed to be wearing a cast; Squinto had an astigmatism. The poem, which began in parody, ended in homage. The poem was a zebra. The poem metabolized regret into immortality. The gene for self-preservation was very assertive in the poem. The poem was the swaddled baby Jesus in a living Christmas crèche. The poem had nothing left for the ritual. The poem was happiest once the last line was read. The poem terminated in a kiss. The poem found you and then you kept finding the poem. The poem was in command of your attention, but the poem belonged to you. The first time you saw the poem was on a poster in your freshman dorm. You meant to call the poem a blowhard, but you said blowhorn—that poem is a real blowhorn. The poem satisfied your taste for repetition. The poem let you greet yourself, arrive at your own door, stand in front of your own mirror. The poem urged you to make a choice while you still could, not to wait so long that you had to make a decision. The poem's fingerprints were on everything that you touched. The poem was your reflection. The poem turned your words into deeds. The poem was the music to the story in your eyes. The poem told you, Avoid Freud—let yourself remain a mystery. The poem survived on your lifesaving breaths. The poem was a bullet that had your name on it. Proverbial was the poem, in case you couldn't tell. How did the poem know you so well? You wondered who gave the poem your telephone number. The poem was the heavy bear that goes with you everywhere. The poem's moon was your moon, too. The poem's letter to you was delivered, despite the fact that its envelope had no stamp. The first time you read the poem aloud, you noticed that it had freshened your breath. The poem looked to you to supply the coda. The poem put a spell on you. The poem put you under the spell of sensuousness. The poem learned your weaknesses. The poem taught you truths. If you split the poem in half, you would have two poems. The poem drummed along with your pulse. The poem surrounded you. The poem stuck out her tongue, blew a raspberry in your face. The poem clarified your thinking on the subject of love and matrimony. You could not offend the poem, try as you might, for the poem had no self-regard. The poem had no mechanism for self-defense. The poem suggested you think more about tomorrow, and forget about today. The poem put an arm around your shoulder, and that warmth caused you to blush. The poem shouldered you into the square ditch. The poem spoke your name and spoke your name and spoke your name and spoke your name until you were a-conjured. You knew the poem before you ever read it. The poem was shining down upon you. The poem planted a smile on your face, which flowered year-round. The poem implored you to reread it. You reread the poem many times because it contained an astonishing truth. Each rereading of the poem paid you new rewards. The poem was on the B-side of the first 45 you ever bought. The poem said to you, If you want to dance, you gotta pay the fiddler. The poem danced and danced and spun you round and round. The poem was written for you. The poem was memorized for you. The poem was anthologized for you. The poem was happy to take your call. The poem lent itself to you. The poem's words knit a sweater for you two sizes too big. Whenever you pet the poem, she would always purr. The poem had a halting speech that was nearly a stammer and, if you had patience, it was endearing as hell. Sidling up on you, that was the poem's way. You wouldn't feel the poem's grip until you were trapped. The poem left you in ruin, just wrecked. The poem, you knew, was one of those snakes with paralyzing yet non-lethal venom. The poem wouldn't kill you. The poem would immobilize you with hypnagogic language. Self-loathing wasn't what you would call the poem. You had to ask, Was the poem seeking heartbreak? In high school, you bullied the poem. The poem told you nothing you didn't already know. The poem begged you to read it aloud. The poem said, I won't steer you wrong. The poem said, I won't give up on you. The poem said, I won't let you down. The poem said, I promise I won't get weird on you. You formed an exhaustion bond with the poem. The poem made you the woman you were meant to be. The poem taught you how to wear a cowboy hat. The subtext of the poem was lost on you. The poem split your imperatives. The poem was looking at you but talking to herself. Say what you want about the poem, but the poem could take a punch. The poem was an escape from your personality. You got a few lines of the poem tattooed on your forearm. Scroll a list of the poem's side effects, and you might not read the poem after all. It was like the poem was making eye contact with you when you read it. If you were to arm wrestle the poem, you would find that the poem was stronger than you could ever have imagined. You join hands with the poem. You walk hand in hand in silence with the poem. The poem taught you how to pray, encouraged prayer as a daily practice. You've read all the essays written about the poem. The poem took your tears and for that you were grateful. You could spit on the poem or put a few coins in his cup. The poem always gave you choices. You say, The poem. You say, The poem. Again, you say, The poem. The poem told you that you were now entered into a binding contract. You could call the poem lazy, but that wouldn't help you win the argument. You could dress the poem up, but you couldn't take her *anywhere*. The poem was the you that only midnight sees. The poem escaped the prison of the page, took refuge in your heart. The poem was your huckleberry friend. The poem was a blotting of you. The poem was a bullet train to your central nervous station. The poem blanketed you in the tension between yellow and blue. The poem pursued the better and—like you— hoped for the best. Sentinel, the poem made you real. The poem was a country music song, if you read it with a twang in your voice. The poem made you laugh, cry, prickle, be silent. The poem made your toenails twinkle. The poem made you understand that your bliss and suffering was forever shared and forever all your own. You stared at the scar on the poem's face. The poem dared you to believe in the unbelievable. The poem dared you to care. Every so often, the poem reminded you to look up at the stars and think about others who might be looking up at the stars. The poem came to tell your faults to you. The poem caught you at being judgmental, which was you at your worst. You asked the poem to tone things down a bit. The poem was an oxeye daisy that you dared to pick. You could hold the poem in one hand. You petitioned the poem to remove certain articles from its constitution. You chased away the poem's livestock. You poisoned the poem's well. When you told your wife, It's the little things that are important, you were talking about the poem. On your fortieth birthday, the poem wished you many happy returns. The poem revitalized your past. Read the poem a hundred times, and you will realize it is totally locked down. How about we make out and I let you play with my tits, said the poem. Frankly, the poem propositioned you, proffered something that, if not, in fact, sexual, could satisfactorily replace your sex life. The poem put a baby inside you. The poem counseled you to let verbs do what verbs do. The poem taught you how to dance, how to kiss a girl, how to heal your broken heart and prepare it for another go. Peace be with you, said the poem. You treasured your time with the poem, every minute of it. Your time spent with the poem was never wasted. In heels, the poem was just as tall as you. The poem sipped a yonic tonic and was transformed into the goddess you know. The poem that you know is actually a revision of the poem. You were the poem's favorite parole officer. The poem said to you, It's just us now. Come, the poem said to you, be my April Fool. The poem kissed you back. The more you looked at the poem, the more you liked it. You thought the poem was good. The fact was, no matter how closely you studied it, no matter how you took it apart, no matter how you broke it down, the poem remained consistent. You believed the poem's heart would beat forever. The poem said, None of you prayed enough. You adored the poem. The poem's beauty scared you. The poem gave you life. The poem gave you purpose. The poem inspired you to write poetry. The poem wanted you to know more about yourself. The poem died for your sins. The poem was you the whole time. You were the poem. And you were the poem. And you and you and you were the poem.

With allusions to Aldrich, Arnold, Auden, Aytoun, Balzary, Barnes, Basho, Baudelaire, Ben-Oni, Berry, Blake, Borges, Brecht, Bronk, Browne, Browning, Carson, Chen, Christie, Colette, Coleridge, de Maupassant, Deutsch, Dickinson, Diogenes, Dryden, Eliot, Emerson, Fenty, Frost, Gibran, Glück, Graves, Gregg, Grimke, Grossman, Hemingway, Herriot, Hirshfield, Hobbes, Hong, Jackson, Jarrell, Johnson, Joudah, Joyce, Keats, King, Larkin, Lorca, Mallarme, Marquis, McKuen, Mitchell, Moore, Nash, Nesbitt, O'Hara, Orr, Paley, Plath, Pound, Ransom, Reed, Rhys, Rogers, Ruefle, Rushdie, Sandburg, Schwartz, Schweitzer, Scott, Shakespeare, Shaw, Shelley, Sontag, Stevens, Sumner, Tate, Teasdale, Tennyson, Thomas, Walcott, Wharton, Whitman, Wilbur, Williams, Willis, Wordsworth, Wright, Yakich, Young, to name but a few.

William Walsh is the author of *The Poets, Forty-five American Boys, ON TV, Questionstruck, Unknown Arts, Without Wax, Pathologies, StephenKing StephenKing*, and *Ampersand, Mass.*

Praise for *The Poems*

"In William Walsh's *The Poems*, the Poem itself is a character, is a plot, is a way in and a way out. The book is an experiment in sound; its musical riffing is a joy to read. It is pithy, open-hearted, rhythmic, seductive, and witty. 'The poem had lost some teeth to years of gnawing. The poem had sturm. The poem had drang,' he says. Drawing on literature, song, newspapers, life, Walsh creates a world all his own, a world where the Poem is king, lover and challenger. It's a singular achievement sustained over 100+ entrancing pages. Let this line be its statement of purpose: 'The poem's resting heartbeat was love.' It's a heartbeat that sounds like your own, and yet is universal."

—Corey Mesler, author of *Memphis Movie* and *The World is Neither Stacked for You nor Against You*

"While the construction of The Poems must be acknowledged—Walsh's skill is undeniable, the use of allusion and other poetic devices masterful—you are immediately in the book, inside its beating, bleeding human heart, and the feeling Walsh's collage of voices creates is something akin to being in love. It is a playful explosion, but also an incantation, a hypnotic spiral; my trance is still lingering. Read it aloud, if you can, and feel the entire world move through you."

—Emily Costa, author of *Until It Feels Right* and *Girl on Girl*

"In *The Poems*, Walsh veers into the oncoming traffic that is hagiography, giving us much less the definition of a poem than its life and the miracles it has performed. 'Yes, the poem was a chancer,' he writes, reminding us that neither saints nor poems live to old age and die surrounded by their families. Walsh gives us the experience of martyrdom, of living and dying by the line."

—Amish Trivedi, author of *FuturePanic* and *Your Relationship with Motion has Changed*

Morant
Roy Goddard

bone bite snare
Michael Mc Aloran

The Face Hole
Gary J. Shipley

Dreams of Amputation
Gary J. Shipley

The Scourge of Villanie
John Marston

Civilisation: Its Cause and Cure
Edward Carpenter

www.ingramcontent.com/pod-product-compliance
Lightning Source LLC
Chambersburg PA
CBHW032019180726
48283CB00008B/2757